Dorrit Willumsen

If It Really Were A Film

translated by Ann-Marie Rasmussen

AN AUGUSTINUS/CURBSTONE BOOK

LC: 82-13655
ISBN: 0-915306-35-2
Danish ISBN: 87-7456-956-2

This publication is supported
by grants from:
Connecticut Commission on the Arts
The Augustinus Foundation
The Danish Government Committee
for Cultural Exchange

cover image: Nia Mason

an Augustinus/Curbstone book

distributed in
Denmark by:

Vindrose Forlag
14 Nybrogade
DK 1203 Copenhagen K

CURBSTONE PRESS
321 Jackson Street Willimantic CT 06226

If It Really Were A Film

The Vestal Virgin

Outside the cry of swallows. They throw themselves into the air, as if they wish they could catch their sharp, little cries. There were peacocks in my grandfather's house and I was fascinated by the beauty of their feathers and by their ugly voices. Ever since we moved away from there I've lived in houses without birds. And I like this house because it's so close to Messalina's house that I only have to stand on my tip-toes to catch a glimpse of the tip of the gable. Then I can imagine her arched nose and arabic eyes.

My mother and her marriages are entirely responsible for the fact that I have lived in so many houses.

I don't remember the first house we lived in. I remember my father as a faint clinking of metal. He looked like a huge shining insect. Supposedly he was also quite handsome, but somehow unreal. Not only because he shone in his breastplate and his leg greaves. But especially because he disappeared in a cloud of dust leaving nothing behind but a few gold coins and some perfume.

The border wars made my parents into a romantic couple. Right up until I was eight years old my father was a hero who had disappeared with his horse and his leg greaves. And my mother was a young, waiting girl.

My mother was very sensitive and beautiful. As soon as someone sang those sentimental songs about lost or returned warriors, she immediately started crying. That's why I don't like music very much. People who wanted to say something nice usually said that my father died a hero. But others were low enough to be of the opinion that he had just stayed away and was living with another woman. And that to top it all off he might come back.

Things like that could provoke my grandmother into making sounds like a peacock. When she wore her most beautiful dress she could resemble a bird, spreading its tail and wings protectively over my mother and me. My grandfather wasn't impressed by things like that. He was old and cynical and he liked gold coins and little children. And I was little enough for him to like me.

Luckily I was a girl like my mother and my grandmother. Because men are mean and deceitful and they use coarse language. And because they're dirty. My grandfather was so filthy that he had to use the public baths. The rest of us washed ourselves in the copper tub. First my grandmother. Then my mother. Then me. And then the cleaner slaves.

I remember that I was happy and satisfied during those eight years. At least I had escaped being a boy, running around with a snotty nose and ears that stuck out.

Suddenly my grandmother died.

Two months later my mother married a young cousin who had worshipped her from afar. That's how he put it. He moved into the house with peacocks to protect my mother. But he moved out again to avoid living with my grandfather. "Two men can't live under one roof," he said. He built his own house and my mother and I moved in with him.

He was very clumsy and nervous. He stammered a little and dropped his eyes when my mother looked at him. In the evening, however, he would court her by positioning himself in the courtyard and bellowing like an ox or meowing like a cat. Perhaps he did this entirely out of consideration for my mother, hoping that she would answer him in one way or another. But she was afraid of the dark and didn't know her way around his house very well. She always started

6

lashing out and screaming. After they had spent four years like that they got divorced.

We lived with my grandfather again for half a year but for some reason his finances, and so my mother's, too, had declined. And she got married again, to my current father, who won't allow me to wear gold sandals because I walk like a cow. Besides which I look like a sack of potatoes. Actually he only started saying that after I got breasts. He can't stand to see me lying crooked at the table. I press his pillows out of shape.

My mother and I borrow the things her husband owns. I realized that one day when I heard someone whisper behind us. "She married and got a house out of it. Not bad, when you consider she has the kid."

Undoubtedly her looks have helped her a great deal. She has a great and indestructable beauty. She can be fat and depressed. And still beautiful. That's why men are happy to lend her a house and possessions. They enjoy her looks and her refined, well-balanced character. In my case their joy is more restrained.

I don't know if she's happy. She looked happy on the day she got married. But that's how she looked at the previous wedding, too.

Sometimes they eat without speaking a word. They only drink little mouthfuls of wine. And they hardly look at one another. Things like that make me feel cold inside.

I think my mother and I were happy with my first father. But I don't remember.

Sometimes I hear Briseis laughing loudly in my current father's room. Sometimes I hear her groaning, like an animal that has been shut in, of course I'm happy it's only Briseis who laughs or groans in that way. The next day her earrings dance just as arrogantly as they usually do.

She does my mother's hair. It's heavy and shiny. She also does mine. And she doesn't understand how I want it. Full and light, as though it had been set that way quite casually. But it shouldn't fall down suddenly, either. She sets it tight and straight. That's how it is, she says. Maybe she's right. My hair isn't like Messalina's hair, which is soft and light and has a faint poppy-colored tinge.

"Her dress slid up.
    Her sandals were purple. Her tunic cherry-red.
    He spread his cloak over her."
Messalina writes that sort of thing on her wax tablet.
When the teacher comes she erases it.
"What are you writing?" he asks.
Messalina doesn't blush.
The teacher glances down at her highly arched feet.
The first day she came to school she went right up to one of the oldest students and asked her to spell the word "lover", so that she would have it if she needed it.
As though she needs to work hard to write.
Everybody likes Messalina and she's used to having things that way. If she notices that someone is a bit reserved with her, she does everything to win that person over. She brings candy. She gives away her bracelets and her rings. Just so that you'll like her.
That's how I got to be her friend. When we met I was just as fascinated by her as everybody else. But since I didn't talk about it Messalina was the one who sought me out.
She started talking about her aunt's new sedan chair. How long it was. How wonderfully upholstered it was. And how you sort of floated along, carried by eight Bithynian slaves dressed in white.
Before I knew it she had asked me to go for a ride in it. And I said yes, even though riding in sedan chairs makes me dizzy. All that movement. The hushed chatter. Looking out and yet not looking out

8

too much, while the city boils up around you and you are carried along by far too many legs.

Actually I didn't think that she would come at all. Still, I put on my best clothes. And at the time we had agreed upon I saw the sedan chair moving through the garden, to the light and measured step of sixteen Bithynian legs.

The aunt, who looked very dignified, almost awe-inspiring with her huge arms pouring out of her dress, went in to my parents. I walked through the garden toward Messalina.

I walked as fast as I could and without watching where I was going. All of a sudden my left foot slipped into a hole while the right one kept on going. And I stumbled forward without trying to break my fall. I heard Messalina scream and I got up to continue towards the chair. She stood right in front of me. She pressed a scarf gently to my lips.

"Did you knock any teeth loose?" she asked.

Only then did I notice that blood was running from my lip, I had skinned my nose and twisted my foot.

I limped back to the house and cleansed the wounds as well as I could.

Later that evening a messenger arrived from Messalina with flowers and cake.

I saved the cake until it was as dry as a piece of wood. When the flowers were almost wilted, I pressed them.

That's what Messalina is like.

Apparently the state is going bankrupt. Messalina and I are buying new clothes. Everybody else is, too. We buy a lot. Because maybe you won't be able to get really elegant clothes in the future. Maybe it won't be possible to buy genuine purple dye and gold ribbon and Greek shoes and oriental silk.

I choose aquamarine blue with silver.

9

Messalina chooses gold and amethyst-colored and melon-colored, green and golden. She tucks up her dress. Her legs are as long as a colt's. Her skin is so golden and soft that you want to touch it.

Messalina wants everything.

She also wants a lion.

She would have its fangs and claws removed. But otherwise she wants it to be completely wild. She would walk it on a golden ribbon. She doesn't think it would harm her. She just thinks it would make her interesting.

If I walked a lion nobody would notice me.

It's not certain either that I'll get married.

I'm not beautiful. But when I look at myself long enough I don't think I'm ugly, either. It's true my cheeks are too broad. And my legs too short.

Messalina is strikingly beautiful. But if I look at her long enough, I can see that there are certain flaws in her looks.

If one looked at us inside it might be the other way around.

By which I don't mean that I have a particularly exquisite skeleton. Or that the bones in Messalina's toes are crooked because she sometimes wears sandals that are too small.

But I imagine that on the inside Messalina is all changing colors and shadows. And yet there are many feelings she doesn't know at all, because people almost always cultivate her in such a friendly, almost deferential way. It's as though she were padded by her own beauty. She is far too confident and secure.

Sometimes I feel like saying something unpleasant to her. But I don't do it. It's far too easy for her to find someone else to show her dresses and bracelets to.

Maybe I'm just envious.

It's rather tiring that I'm only praised for my modesty. Particularly because I know that it is just as self-assertive and deliberate as Messalina's pleasant disposition.

And what is modesty, really? To know that I have less right to everything than Messalina?

And why? Why is it that way?

The days when my brother, or more correctly my third father's son, is here are the worst. He is eighteen and studies law. But you never see him with a book. He goes to the circus and to the theater. Every morning he runs around Mars Field seven times just to keep in shape. And he puts his excellent shape to use by strolling through the colonnades and whistling softly and flatteringly at the girls.

He's studying people, he says. My mother doesn't care. My father nods approvingly. Otherwise my brother is envious of me because I can still live at home and he can't.

He doesn't hide the fact that he knows it's my mother's fault. She won't have him in the house because of his violent temper.

Boy's can't be taught anything.

Actually he is good-looking. Has a rare blondish cast to his hair. I like to see him move. His movements are so free. His eyes shine and at times he acts as though he's been drinking wine in the morning. He teases me about my fat cheeks. I look like a tomcat, he says. And that makes me furious. I pull his hair.

I hate him.

I try to eat as little as possible. And I still look fat.

He eats like a beast of prey and is still sleek and thin.

He can only be completely quiet if I tell him about Messalina, or if she is visiting.

Of course Messalina is getting married first, even though she is half a year younger than me. But then I wouldn't be very pleased with the match. He is distinguished but rather old.

Some people say that she thought about running away. But that she gave the idea up. She couldn't plan anything and she didn't know which dresses to take along, either.

My parents sent their best wishes to the wedding. I gave her my most beautiful ring.

A few weeks later she invited me to see the presents and the house.

She was sumptuously dressed in peach, black and gold. But somehow she seemed different.

She had her lion.

It was very playful and spoiled. You could stroke its fat, soft back. That was like stirring warm honey with your hand. You didn't need to be afraid that it might scratch. Its paws were still bandaged in yellow silk after its claws had been pulled out. Messalina hadn't been able to bear its wailing while that had been done. She went to the countryside with her husband. It had also been castrated on account of the smell, and its fangs had been removed.

We played with it for a long time. It has a sleepy, totally enchanting look. Messalina can hardly wait for it to grow up and have a mane.

In the garden we met her husband.

He greeted us in a friendly and accomodating way. But it was as though we were both strangers. It almost seemed as though he was introducing himself to Messalina.

She turned and watched him walk away. I think it hurt her that he didn't pay more attention to her in front of me. They didn't act as though they were married at all. At least not as I'd imagined it as far as Messalina was concerned.

Later we sat in the shade and ate cake and drank wine. Messalina talked about the party and the presents and the trip.

I would have liked to ask what it was like.

Whether he spread his cloak over her.

Whether her dress slid up.

I looked down at her feet.

She smiled.

The air smelled as though it were spiced with marjoram and cloves. And with her heavy, dry perfume. For one reason or another I suddenly realized that I had never heard Messalina say anything unpleasant.

We kissed each other on the cheek and said good-bye. Before we had never kissed when we parted.

On my way home I had a frightening experience.

Suddenly I felt a hard blow on my shoulder. A rooftile that had come loose shattered at my feet and the dust swirled up into my eyes and hair.

I opened my mouth. But I didn't scream. I brushed myself carefully and kept on going.

As I turned the corner, I heard terrible screams and a deafening explosion. The top floor of the house was whirling through the air. People and masonry smashed to the earth. Later I heard that at least twenty were hurt and two died. One an old woman, the other a child.

If I had screamed loud, as a warning, when the tile hit me. Maybe it wouldn't have happened. Some of them would undoubtedly have made it out. But I just kept quiet and kept on going after brushing my clothes.

Of course I'm not the person who built the house. Of course it happens now and again that a house collapses. And I don't own the building and it's not my fault that the masonry is rotten.

But still—if only, at that moment, I'd had a wild, aggressive, warning scream.

Right now my parents are considering the possibilities for getting me married. I can tell by the way they look at me. They don't seem very optimistic. Maybe I don't want it to work out, either. But I don't know what I really want. So I can't give an opinion if I should be asked.

Maybe I'm better suited to being a married man's mistress. He could visit me once a week. The other days I could miss him and be free.

The housekeeping would be quite simple. However I'm not suited to doing much myself or to telling others what to do. So it would be more fitting in that way, too. But unfortunately I don't know any married man who has suggested that sort of arrangment to me. And the plans my parents are making aren't that immoral. They intend only the best for me, they say.

I can see two possibilities for marriage.

One is the son of the greengrocer. He delivers our groceries. He's tall, his skin is golden like Messalina's legs. He moves as freely and easily as my brother does.

When we are having fruit and vegetables delivered I sit in the garden. I turn my profile towards him. Because I am most presentable in profile. And I appear somewhat proud.

We've never spoken.

The other possibility is my brother's friend.

When he's here my brother doesn't tease me. On the other hand his friend does. But in a different way. He looks straight at me. And I look at him. His hands are broad and bony. His body is stocky. But his features are regular and nice-looking and his hair shines as black as raven's feathers.

When he is here I smile a lot. But I'm not interested in him and actually I don't like to smile.

I like actors best.

But of course I can't marry an actor. I can't even send them flowers or fruit. I can only sit on the cold bench and listen to the beauty of their voices and cry when they die.

I like their high-heeled shoes. And their masks and make-up which make them seem either very masculine or very fragile and feminine.

Their voices are high and beautiful. The words become so whole that one can almost touch them.

In particular I love the one who plays Medea. And I'm not alone in that. Once the guards had to protect him so that the audience couldn't crowd onto the stage and tear his clothes and hair. I wanted to also. But I practiced restraint and contented myself with screaming.

Once I saw him on the street. His eyebrows were plucked and dyed as painstakingly as a woman's. His naked temples made me feel tenderness.

It was so startling that he wasn't as perfect as on stage. That his clothing wasn't splendid and gleaming, that his gestures weren't at all compelling, though his hands still possessed that extended pain when he handled the vegetables and the fruit.

I followed him at a distance, shocked and warmed by his otherness. And by my otherness. Because suddenly I knew that I wished I were a man and an actor.

"Smile," says my mother when we are at the circus.

And I smile during the procession when the statues of the gods are being carried in. I smile when the emperor takes his seat and the sun makes his face shine.

This year I can see everything because everybody is supposed to see me. But really it's no use. After all, who would want a girl who turns pale and holds smelling salts under her nose? Once you're nauseous it doesn't matter much that you're wearing aquamarine blue.

I like the races because of the speed, the colors and the beauty of the horses. But the gladiator fights and the smell of the wild animals, flesh ripping open, bodies straining to the limit only to stiffen suddenly and be dragged off. I wish I could get out of seeing that.

Of course I'm relieved that I'm not the one who is dying. But at the same time it's rather embarrassing that this sort of display doesn't make me really sick. Usually just pricking myself on a needle makes me faint. And really it's rather indifferent of me that I've gotten so used to seeing gladiators, lions and bears killed that I don't even get a fever.

I try glancing over at Messalina. She's easy to find. Her eyes are sparkling. It's as though she only sees life and movement. And as though she thinks the colors of blood and entrails are wonderful. When the dead are being dragged out, she fans herself or eats lozenges.

She doesn't see me. She and her husband are sitting close to the emperor. She is radiant in her silk and her jewels. And I'm just a girl with a puckered-up mouth and smelling salts under my nose.

Everyone seems so excited, even aroused. As though the killing gives them some sort of freedom. Even my mother follows a handsome driver with her eyes, as he strolls past with a ridiculous, arrogant look on his face.

And then a very elegant lady gets up from one of the most distinguished seats and makes her way down to the most common ones. Her husband and children turn around and watch her in amazement.

She disappears in the crowd with a heavy, sweating gladiator. He killed a bear which had wounded him in the shoulder. At that moment there was a kind of brutal, aggressive beauty in his movements. Now he jogs along, bowlegged and a little pudgy beside her. She examines his wound with interest. She flares her sensitive nostrils, as though blood mixed with sweat gives off a special aroma. But how will she return?

Maybe she is just as tragic as Medea. But I don't feel that. Because I can't imagine that Jason sweated or was bowlegged.

No. I look forward to the real tragedies. The ones on stage. I can cry about them.

16

Afterwards I'm completely cleansed. It's as though everything has become completely different. Even the cloth of my dress, the mirror, my own face and the jars in the kitchen.

At the dinner table I have to talk about it, keep on talking about it. I try to make the words come out of my mouth as beautifully as the actors do.

My gestures become grand and exaggerated. I almost knock over the glasses. But I can't stop, even though they say I'm making a fool of myself. My brother and his friend make fun of me. And I can tell that even Briseis thinks I'm ridiculous.

But it's as though the words and gestures make me into a different person.

Of course things had to turn out this way.

I have written too much on my wax tablets and read too many books. But in particular I made too much of a fool of myself at the dinner table. Even my eyes look ridiculous, they say. And for that reason they think I'm philosophical or religious.

They have consulted the time of my birth and my stars. They have paid an old woman to stare at my left palm.

The stars, my palm and the old woman. All of it indicates that I am well-suited to becoming a vestal virgin.

I feel like drawing new lines on my hand. I feel like kicking the old woman in the stomach or at least pulling my hand away and clenching it. I think she knew. Because she kept on mumbling something about an early and dishonorable death, as though she were the one who decided everything. I regret not pulling her moustache. I could have done that, if nothing else.

But they consider me well brought up and insignificant so if I did something like that they would think I was crazy. But I'm not crazy. I just don't like change. Things like that make me restless. I wake up at the wrong time and fall asleep at the wrong time. My hair goes every which way. There are days that crumble away. And things that suddenly crowd in. My jewelry. The little make-up jars, the mirror in its carved frame. My tame bird and the blue dress that didn't bring me happiness, anyway.—Everything I am fond of and can't take with me.

At night I tip-toe down to the kitchen and drink strong, heady wine. I drink until my tongue feels raw and swollen.

But it doesn't help.

Sometimes Nape, our oldest slave, wakes up, she looks at me and shakes her head.

Messalina says I should run away.

But where to?

Is there anyone waiting with a sedan chair or a rope ladder or just a stiff-legged horse?

Messalina says I could easily get the greengrocer's son or my brother's friend. Anybody at all, she says and smiles.

Messalina with her lion. Her funny, old husband and her lovers.

Because she doesn't make a secret of anything.

They go in and out of her house.

They drink the house wine and eat fruit from the garden. They assure Messalina that she is irresistible.

Her husband doesn't know. Or he acts as though he doesn't know. Maybe he's deceiving her more than she's deceiving him.

She has had her first child, a soft chubby-faced boy with velvet eyes. She plays with him and caresses him the way she used to caress the lion with soft paws. He smells acidy and warm.

Messalina's purple dress moves like a flame. She still has dimples and eyes that search far.

Affirmation is what she's searching for. A mirror.

And men come to her with their warmth and their confusion. With their confidences and their hasty declarations of love. Messalina's sex is an open wound, always demanding the laying on of hands, and caresses.

But if the poisonous mushrooms don't work. If the sacrifices at the Isis temple don't work. If the restlessness in her sex is no longer caused by desire—well, then she's alone.

In the temple of the vestal virgins I'd never end up in Messalina's situation. The imposed chastity alone would prevent me from having to sneak through the narrow alleys behind the marketplace to find some witch or procuress who would give me a jar of vinegar or some other drink that induces miscarriage, in exchange for a purse full of gold coins.

Or maybe I would rather have worshipped a different god. For example have been a priestess of Isis. Then I would meet Messalina every time she came to pray for a quick and relatively painless abortion. Maybe I could present her case to the goddess with special emphasis. But the Isis temple isn't a very solid concern. It might be just a part of the oriental boom.

Many of the male gods are interesting. But unfortunately men are worshipped by men. And women by women. At least if it's supposed to be serious. I can't, for example, bring myself to join the worship of Priapus. I can't dance. And I would find it terribly embarassing to flap around with the god's leather phallus. Either I would blush or I'd start laughing. Or maybe both.

My parents are probably right in thinking that it's best I be employed in a solid, state-run enterprise. The times are unsure. But after all, since the temple of Vesta guards the hearth of the city, there probably won't be any cut-backs there.

I'll resign myself. Even though it's never been my job to kindle the fire, I'm sure I can figure out how to guard the flames. And I'll devote my life to worshipping this head-housewife figure, even though I never considered keeping house.

How I wish the temple were warm. It's as though even the fire is somehow chilly and abstract in here. We never really let it blaze up. We just keep a little tame flame burning. The air outside can be as warm and soft as cat fur. But the temple's walls are like ice.

The food is monotonous and the wine weak. Yet still I was so afraid in the beginning that we wouldn't be given enough food that just the smell of cooking aroused my senses. I ate every meal as though I could eat my way to security. I didn't think about my breasts or my cheeks.

But now I've started losing weight.

I'm still quite nervous. I can tell by my hands. When I reach for something they tremble the way birds do. Of course that's not very practical. But nobody says anything about it.

Actually I'm a little frightened of being together with the other women. I'm watching and waiting, I'm not trying to please. Because I'm afraid they will hate me later.

The duties of a priestess aren't as difficult as I had imagined they would be. There are others with trembling hands and one with a crooked hip. And yet we have been chosen to keep house for Vesta, or perhaps first and foremost for ourselves.

And aside from the business with my hands and my tendency to look ridiculous, I seem so unusually ordinary that nobody believes I could make provoking or unusual mistakes in the ceremony or in the daily care of the goddess.

Besides all of us are a little strange. Little Clodia who talks and talks. About how her brother fell out of a chariot and broke his neck. About how her sister died during her seventh pregnancy. And the mother poisoned a younger brother because he made an older cousin pregnant. But the father discovered it and may have killed the mother and certainly would have married the cousin if he hadn't got water in his lungs and been drowned from the inside a year later. She laughs the whole time she's speaking, a cheerful, fluttering laughter. As though laughter can make all the misfortunes disappear.

Hermione has a long, delicate face. She is totally, transparently pale, as though all her color had gone up in smoke. She has studied philosophy. Now she uses her talent for Vesta. When she speaks, Vesta shines chaste, bright and very clear. Hermione's thoughts are pillars and long roads of white polished marble.

Pompeia moves like a boy. Her hands are long and narrow and very elegant. Sometimes she presses her fingertips together when she's thinking about something. But otherwise that is the only feminine, hesitating gesture I have seen her make. Occasionally she picks her nose. It's as though she never thinks about her movements. She walks right into the room without even glancing in the mirror. Her voice, which is slightly husky, has an eager, leaping quality. Her voice and her hands. Just her finger, on its way to her nose, makes me feel warm. But I can't find anything to say. I can hardly move when I'm close to her. Because even though I think about being graceful, I'm clumsy beside her.

When we were picking apples, she had picked seven baskets before I had filled a half. She climbed around in the trees. Our headmistress saw her from the window. Pompeia radiated such pleasure during the apple harvest that she was fired from that job. Instead she had to polish silver in the kitchen.

The headmistress has served Vesta the longest and therefore she is the most distinguished and virtuous of us all. She has an unusually ugly voice. But she speaks and sings very loudly, as though she were equipped with a beautiful voice. If Vesta really has listened to her all these years she can't be much of a lover of beauty.

Maybe it's a sign of sympathy that the headmistress always touches

21

my shoulder when she speaks to me. Her hands are large and warm. They feel like cow tongues through my clothes. And I hunch my shoulders as though I were folding myself into my shoulders in a particularly chaste way. That's how I try to show my disgust.

At the marketplace I pull my veil tight across my face. And even though the white wool gown makes me look older and is poorly cut, I still hear people calling me "the little vestal virgin" or "the beautiful vestal virgin". And it flatters me, even though it's useless, of course.

Some follow me all the way through the colonnades. Whispering and mumbling about their desire, which is only the consciousness that I am untouchable, am something especially challenging.

I'll probably never see Messalina again.

Poor Messalina. She's become empress because her husband has become emperor.

How will she cope with that?

It's still a time of crisis. But I don't keep up with politics much. Fires, border wars, murder, demolition of houses—things like that only reach us as rumors. They have no direct connection to us.

We only notice the bad times because we have too much to do. People stream to the temples to pray and ask advice.

The economy is bad. We pour a jar of wine on the ground and chop the heads off some doves and chickens to prove that there is no reason to be afraid.

The temple is decorated with flowers. And our gowns are made of new white wool. We move conscientiously in very involved processions. We look solemn and peaceful. We answer reassuringly and wisely, we try at least to give an answer which holds out some promise.

Inside ourselves we all know that we don't do anything special. That everything is disintegrating. That some people don't have money or bread and that it doesn't help them very much when we guard the

22

city's hearth, with its fire that burns without giving off warmth.

Yesterday the entire imperial family came to the temple. The place was packed with people. They hung onto the walls and in the trees. And the garden was trampled. Apparently they believed that their prayers and sacrifices had greater value if the emperor participated in them.

For the first time since I came here, I saw Messalina. She stood far away from me. But still I hoped she would notice me.

She has become plumper. Her laziness in front of the make-up mirror could be seen on her face. She had the hint of a double chin. But her whole body radiated gentle, melancholy grace. Her gestures, her long, heavy, made-up eyes overflowed with the deepest anxiety, which was emphasized by pearl earrings. How her little, nervous mouth moved me. This wistful, sad empress who exerted herself so much to find a solution to the state's problems that her eyes swam with tears.

I wished that a miracle would happen. Just for her sake.

Suddenly I could see from her face that it happened. She smiled a big, arrogant, slightly ferocious smile.

I saw Messalina's miracle.

He stood at the back of the temple with his hood pulled over his head, as though he were trying to hide.

He is very young. I've heard that he is supposed to be both articulate and charming.

Messalina left the temple without seeing me. She has probably forgotten about me long ago. And I think of her every day. Apparently I'm the one who gets the most out of our friendship.

Perhaps it's the rumors about Messalina which make my hands tremble so badly that I drop things if I don't concentrate on holding on to them.

Every time I go to market I hear new gossip about her.

She has three lovers.

They don't crawl in the window. They have themselves announced at the front gate of the house.

What can she see in the squat soldier with a damp lower lip and little, deep-set eyes? He's probably got scars all over his body and besides he has less hair than her husband.

What does she see in the law student who wears Greek shoes?

Or the fat attorney, whom even the ugliest slave girl runs away from? Perhaps it's his sedan chair with violet silk pillows and so many gold tassels that its splendor outdoes even the imperial one? He probably acquired it just to camouflage the fact that by now it takes twenty slaves to haul his fat around town.

If I wrote a letter. If I warned her, told her that at the very least she shouldn't go to rendevous wearing a gold cloak. That at the very least she shouldn't have any more abortions at the procuress's behind the marketplace. That she shouldn't get drunk and talk too much. That she must lie, no matter what, if someone questions her.

Messalina would laugh.

Or even worse. She might show the letter to her husband and laugh.

Messalina is so depraved that she is totally innocent.

If she hadn't been born into such a distinguished family, she would probably have become one of these gentle courtesans who stands on the street at night in their thin silk dresses and blond wigs, elegantly made-up and with tired eyes.

She would never save enough money to buy a shop.

Gold ignites itself in Messalina's hands.

Messalina doesn't keep accounts. She dreams on soft cushions in the shade or in rooms where the sun can't make her make-up run.

Her blue-green eyelids resemble the skin of a delicate snake.

Messalina bathes in rose petals and allows herself to be massaged in oil made from fresh almonds.

24

Her body is lazy, sweet-smelling and soft.

Messalina is charged with the eroticism around her. And everyone talks about her disintegration and decline in order to avoid talking about their own. Or perhaps to talk about themselves in an indirect, less binding fashion.

Perhaps I think about her so much because I still haven't become attached to any of the other women. I run away from Clodia's laughter and from the headmistress's hands. Hermione's thoughts tire me. Perhaps I would like to be united with Pompeia's movements and listen to her leaping voice. But how can I approach movements which are forbidden?

I fold into myself.

Like a blade that is folded until it is nothing but quivering and sharpness. And yet the edge seems so soft, even when you only graze it.

I look at my legs.

A pair of depressing, white legs. Not the sort of legs one would want to touch. But I touch them myself to comfort them in their loneliness. Or to warm them. To warm my entire body. Sometimes I feel as cold as the stone woman in the fountain. When I open my mouth, I expect a thin stream of water to pour out.

That's why I touch myself while I think about Messalina, who sighs from the heat. Messalina, who allows herself to be fanned by long ostrich feathers. Messalina, who never sleeps alone. But wraps herself around the bodies of men, children and lions.

Empress Messalina, who gives orders.

Empress Messalina, who sneaks behind the marketplace with a purse in her hand.

The empress, who is carried to the temple. She seems to be praying for the state. But she is so fervent because she is praying for herself.

The days when I am assigned to market duty are the best. I allow myself lots of time, as though I can't find flowers, vegetables or bread that are worthy of the temple.

I go to the places where there are the most people. I even pass by the slave market. And I do that even though I can't bear to see anyone whipped or suffer any physical injury. It makes me feel as though my skin is curling up. And I'm ashamed of it.

When I was a child I ran away from things like that. Even at the circus games I only watched with my hands pressed in front of my eyes. Now I walk here as though I wished to subject myself, on purpose, to the things I despise. I see the tall, barbarian women with their broad faces and large, proud mouths that seem to be able to swallow everything or spit on everything. Some stoop. Others look straight ahead with light, shining eyes, as if they haven't grasped what is going on. I see the tall, slim Bithynians, and Phoenicians with beautiful noses. Once in a while one of them is wearing a valuable ring. And one knows that he or she was born to be something else, but that the course of their life has been broken, suddenly and completely meaninglessly. Maybe because of a bad star or a particular line in their hand. Maybe an old, ugly woman told them a long time ago that it would happen. But they thought she was wrong. That they could avert fate with a sacrifice or maybe commit suicide when misfortune struck.

Anyone can see that what goes on here is unnatural.

That they all ought to be free this instant.

But then who would carry our sedan chairs? Tie our sandals? Cultivate the earth? And cook the food?

If they were free, we would immediately fall socially. Maybe there wouldn't be enough food, if they were going to eat their fill as well. In any case, there certainly wouldn't be roast birds, wild boar meat, bread or wine for all of us.

We know that they will rebel one day and take the houses, the gold, the birds, our hair, maybe our heads and the silk. But we wait. Maybe it will last one more day. Maybe one year. Maybe fifty years or more.

In the meantime the men fill their houses with gold, silver and statues of bronze and marble. Sometimes there isn't even room for all of it in the house, they have to cram it into the cellar.

The women are radiant with the beauty they buy. The long, golden wigs from the barbarian women. The straight, black hair from Egypt.

And they all desire even more gold, more silver, more silk and more shining stones.

We acquire tame lions and fierce dogs to guard against slaves and thieves.

And when we feed the dogs with raw meat or cautiously pet the lion, we seem almost gentle.

Today I've been here for one year.

My mother has visited me three times. Each time she has watched me with her sad, dark-brown look, as though she blames me for not being more pleased with her visits or my existence.

I have watched her, my look just as sad, just as dark-brown. Perhaps she thinks I blame her for the decision to put me here. And I do to a certain degree.

She hasn't mentioned my father or my brother.

They haven't been here, either.

My grandfather is dead, she says. Maybe I should have asked for permission to visit him.

After his death he has haunted me a great deal. He is very little and has sunken cheeks like an exposed child.

Once when I was little I sought refuge in his bed during a thunderstorm. I saw his sex under the tunic. "That must be the thing they call his hernia," I thought.

27

My mother and I talk about the fountain, the peach trees and the weather. Once she also remarked on the cold.

We observe each other like two strangers. And suddenly we get up and kiss each other good-by with relief..

If only I were dead instead of Messalina.

If only I had warned her. If for no other reason than for the sake of my conscience.

What I always feared has finally happened. Messalina was so alive that she had to die. But I, who live so little, will probably have to continue doing so for a long time.

An emperor in times of crisis can't afford to have a wife who disgraces him. She is supposed to increase his dignity or give him dignity if he lacks it.

But I don't believe it could be her husband who has exposed her or demanded revenge.

Perhaps it was someone she refused.

But she never refused anyone. She was too gentle.

The person in question must have done it out of pure malice or in hopes of attaining some prestige or reward for exposing what everybody already knew.

But by what right can one spy on an empress in a park when she is in the middle of sexual intercourse?

Now one of her lovers has been executed. Two others have fled. They didn't help her.

Messalina was supposed to save her honor, or more correctly the emperor's honor, by committing suicide. A trial would have made the whole business comical. But she would have preferred the comical.

How do they know at the marketplace that her hand trembled and she couldn't find her heart. It must have been far too easy to find at the moment. Ready to fly out of her body like a bird.

But she couldn't do it. They had to help her wield the knife. She didn't defend herself. But she resisted when they guided her hand. How could they do it? Messalina's hands. They are small and oval—perfectly formed and with bitten nails.

He was a fugitive. He stumbled in his ridiculous Greek shoes. And when I met him he was neither particularly charming nor articulate. I had seen him in the temple before. That's why I thought he brought a message from her. Maybe she told him my name once. Maybe she called it out. Maybe it was just Vesta she called on.

He came in great confusion. He came with his shivering, his nervous sweat and his breathlessness.

He expected me to calm him down. And suddenly I understood how much restlessness Messalina must have received. How many confused, broken words.

His sex swung against my hip. I wasn't used to that. The sex of the gods is calm, made of marble or gold or at least of leather.

He touched my loins as though he wanted to wash himself in me. As though he wanted to sink into me as if into water.

I bit him on the throat so that I wouldn't scream.

He sucked on my ear so that he wouldn't groan.

The vaulting of the cellar shut us in.

It was her name he mumbled. It was her we cried over. And not our own sudden love or sorrow, as we tried to pretend so as not to hurt each other more than was necessary.

The cellar was very cold. It was as though the earth had closed itself around us. For a moment we were still, then he hurried away. I don't know why he came specifically to me.

But it seemed as though it were her life I had lived. As though she had been a large, reckless and ferocious line of breakers. And I was just a little wave that had rippled along beside her.

I went up to the others. I wrung out a rag in ice-cold water. It was the day for washing Vesta's pillars and steps. And I participate in Vesta's ordinary housekeeping.

I dream that my nose has become the snout of a beast of prey. I move my hand over my face. It's as usual. But I have suddenly acquired an animal's sense of smell.

Marjoram. Basil. Fennel. The smells from the garden rush into my room and attack me.

As soon as we lie down at the table, I feel nauseous. I let the serving dishes wander past. Only once in a while do I let a piece of bread or some fruit slide down into the folds of my gown. Just so that my lack of appetite won't be too noticable.

Market duty is unbearable.

I can't understand that it's the same marketplace.

Everything stinks.

The fish smell rotten and dead. The earthy smell of the vegetables rushes in on me. And the peaches and the pears must be spoiled, even though they don't have any spots.

The day before yesterday I had to hide because the sight of dead rabbits made me throw up. Afterwards I ate lemons with the peel and the seeds without as much as washing them first.

I can't even get close to smoked meat. The sun burns down on the cages with the poultry. And I'm certain that the hens have both mites and lice.

People sweat. Their smell makes me furious. I feel like kicking them in the shins or stepping hard on their sour, diseased toes.

"These dahlias can't possibily be fresh," I say to the flower shop keeper.

He looks astonished.

If I weren't wearing this gown, he would tell me off and say that I could take my business elsewhere.

I know now that all of my gentle, modest nature was just a kind of alchemy—a fleeting condition, which was changed the day he deposited his seed and his restlessness between my legs.

Sometimes I walk down the alleys Messalina crept through at night. I know where the procuress lives. At night the dull-green light flows out of her window onto the alley. During the day it's dark. But I can sense the smell of her liquids and dried mushrooms. You rarely meet anyone there.

Just once I was spoken to by a young woman.

She was very young and thin, dressed in a peach-colored silk dress with gold borders which were unraveling around her feet. Her hair shone red.

She turned towards me with bright eyes, and her skin was dirty and dissolved like a wall which is stained with moisture.

She stretched out her palm towards me.

At first I thought she wanted me to read her hand. Then I realized that she was begging and I shook my head and pointed to my gown, to indicate that I have no personal property.

She started laughing.

Her laughter was shrill and ugly.

"How sick," she laughed. "I've never seen anything so sick before."

I hurried away.

Later I realized that it was my chastity she was laughing at.

The other vestals have also noticed my condition. Little Clodia talks even more than usual, as if the misfortunes of her family and her light chattering could sweep away my fate.

My matronly figure makes Pompeia shy. My heavy, clumsy movements make her stiffen. She presses the tips of her fingers together or picks her nose in a melancholy and thoughtful fashion. But yesterday at dinner she suddenly touched my hand. It was a warm and firm handclasp. As though she were promising me something and I didn't know what it was. I ate almost normally for the rest of the meal.

Hermione disappears like a shadow when she sees me. My condition isn't found in her philosophy.

It's obvious that everybody knows it and also that everybody knows what will happen. Sometimes I hear their simmering whispers and when I enter, there is total silence, as though they were ashamed or afraid.

I know that their silence is a warning about the moment when they must follow the laws of the temple and really bury me alive.

And I understand their embarassment. I wouldn't want to be in their place.

Clodia tells me that my brother has come to visit. She leads him into the room and leaves the door open, as though to indicate the most obvious possibility for flight.

My brother looks pale and agitated. It seems odd to me that he, too, has grown older.

"Come on," he says, "you have to run away."

But I remain seated and shake my head. I'm totally worn out. I've thought about it hundreds of times. How easily I could slip through the gate. How I could replace this gown. How I could settle somewhere or other. But where? And as what? As a prostitute maybe, if anybody would pay for my body. And the child—would it be exposed? And how far does one have to run? No, I can't go on.

"I want you out of this house!" he screams and paces up and down the room.

"You should have thought of that earlier," I say, not without bitterness.

"It's not my fault," he says angrily, as though everything still centered on him.

I start smiling. And he pulls me up by my hair and slaps me a few times in the face, as though I were a horse he wanted to set in motion. My cheeks smart. But to my surprise I don't start crying.

I feel pity for him, because after all he has come here for my sake.

"Let's be friends," I say and touch his arm.

"Only if you come with me. I won't be the friend of a person who is both dead and dishonored."

Since I just shake my head and remain standing, he tears himself away and rushes out the door.

The headmistress touches me with her big, damp hands. I don't hunch my shoulders.

"You know the laws of Vesta," she says.

I am content to nod. Because it would be far too difficult to admit that I have broken the vow of chastity to end up in my present condition. And that I am perfectly well aware that the oblong hole they have been busy digging is intended for me.

Perhaps I could avoid it by inventing some elaborate story about the conception having come about with the help of a god. Perhaps I could save my life that way. But I've almost forgotten everything I once knew about the male gods, so it would be hard for me to make the story sound believable. And besides the child would grow up with an obligation to do something miraculous. And a child of mine, fathered by a random law student, will hardly seem particularly divine.

She is still clasping my shoulders when she starts sobbing, first darkly and gutturally, then violently and gratingly. Big tears run down her cheeks.

I don't know if she is crying for me or if she feels ashamed in the presence of the goddess. But after I've seen the gravel I feel, for the first time, a little expectant and arrogant, as though it were something

33

I had decided myself. The earth has such a raw and cool smell, and I think of all the houses I've lived in, and the time I fell because I was going for a ride in a sedan chair with Messalina.

They will probably hold on to my arms. But I won't resist. The moment they let me go, I'll fall over backwards by myself. I'll shut my eyes tight and not think about worms and insects.

They will probably shovel slowly, hoping to hear a regret or a scream. But how should I be able to feel repentance? I've always done what they expected. Others left their mark on me. They did it so emphatically and so often that my true nature has been lost. And my face value is theirs. I will become a plot of ground they don't walk on and a bitter taste in their mouths. I won't think about Vesta's white, marble eyes or about the perfect sex of the gods. I will think about the dampness in the cellar and about the man who came to me a fugitive in peril because of Messalina's death. On that day I was far more moved, that day I understood that I had lived through her.

A Couple

The shadows of the trees glide over him as if they would like to erase him. The grass bends under the soles of his shoes. Everything is movement.

That's how it was that evening, too.

He saw them in the grass together. Their bodies were wet and smooth as if they had been washed up from some far-away coast. Their eyes were closed tightly, like the eyes of sleeping children. He noticed the wrinkles around Lea's eyelids.

He didn't think of them as his wife and his friend.

He didn't connect the sleepers with words like intercourse, infidelity, adultery.

The fragile skin around their hips filled him with tenderness for an instant.

He went in.

Maybe he should have shouted.

Maybe they would have pressed themselves even closer together. Maybe they would have started up like birds.

He did nothing.

But the image. The intertwined bodies. The closed eyes. It all remained somewhere inside of him.

Inside everything is in its place. The table. The sofa. The washing machine. The beds. The clothing shut into closets.

The lights are on. But there aren't any guests.

Lea moves from room to room.

Her fumbling, yielding, soft, self-effacing movements. Her do-you-like-me movements. Her it-doesn't-matter movements. Her dream breasts. Her big, obscene smile.

No. There's nothing special about her. Her colors are sparrow-like. At times her movements are clumsy.

But suddenly she behaves as though she were irresistable, interesting. She has no middle register. No transition from self-effacing to provocative. From shy to pushy. Nothing ordinary.

Lea in white. The high-heeled, skinny shoes. The slenderness of her legs. Her nervous fidgeting. Her expectant fidgeting.

And her hair is smooth and glossy and loose. Dark with a streak of blond, almost white hair at her left temple.

He should never have asked.

The words made the intertwined bodies into something dubious.

The words trapped them in a net of explanations, clarifications, allegations.

"I wasn't in love with him," she said. "But he acted like he expected it. And I didn't want to be a cock-tease."

He laughed. Was it the bitterness in his own laughter that hurt him? Or was it her matter-of-fact attitude?

And later her sinner's pose: "Well, if it means so much to you I won't do it anymore."

But how can making a limited area of skin taboo prove faithfulness or loyalty?

And freedom, Lea's personal freedom. Was it liberation or conventionality that caused her to unbutton? Or did she do it out of desire after all?

And how often? How? With whom?

He knows that she lies.

He's often heard her lie on the telephone.

"Sorry—My husband isn't home right now.—I'm expecting him in an hour. But he might not return until tomorrow.—I'm afraid I just can't say for sure."

He'd asked her to do it himself. He was in the bathtub or reading the paper and he admired her because she lied so believably.

But now.

"I thought—You said—We agreed—You meant—I assumed—But you didn't say—And I might have meant anyway."

Lying—is it only part of the truth?

In the lines of her body? In the waves of her hair? In a little, tiny part of her brain? Can it be read in her palm? Or in the small, broken screams when he runs his nails over her skin? Is the truth there?

The truth.

It doesn't exist.

There is only the truth about.

Buzzing like a fly. A droning through sleep. And you stretch out your hand to catch it and crush it. But the hand stops. It's too disgusting.

When they met they were certain that they wouldn't get married. He was twenty-six and still a student. He wanted to be at least thirty before he got tied down. The world was waiting for him.

Lea didn't believe in marriage.

She'd never seen it work out, she said.

She wasn't being coy when she said that. And really it wasn't the idea of being unhappy that frightened her. Whenever she had fallen in love before she had been unhappy in some way or another. She didn't so much want a stable relationship, either. Rather, she wanted to be high on some feeling. And she was certain that the routine of a marriage would cause her feeling to burn out about as fast as a match.

When Dan met her she had just turned twenty. She was working in a laboratory where she did analyses of soaps and creams without having any particular sense of precision.

She was still shaken and tense after an affair with a fifty-five year old man who went to bed with her because his wife got pregnant with someone else. She told about how she was supposed to have been his fifth virgin. But she didn't have a hymen. Maybe she had deflowered herself as a child. She wondered about how that could have happened, and why it should be important to him. She was like a spectator to her own actions.

But in the theater and at the movies her feelings flickered up.

All the big love scenes. All the romantic couples. Romeo and Juliet. Tristan and Isolde. Pelleas and Melisande. She wasn't even musical. She went for the sake of the plot.

"Emotional pornography," thought Dan.

"I'm never going to get married." she mumbled.

She wanted to be self-supporting and romantic.

The smell of diaphram jelly filled the room.

A year later they were married.

Had he mistaken her accommodating nature for maturity?

And she, a person who had always looked for fathers. Doctors, teachers, executives. They could be bald, stiff-legged and married. They could suffer from digestive problems and migraine headaches. She even saw their shortcomings in a romantic light. Occasionally, she had tried, without success, to transfer her feelings to their young, arrogant sons. Or she had struck up friendships with their daughters, whom she never had anything in common with, anyway.

Was it because she wanted to insure herself against the future?

Or did she see a kind of father in Dan's beautiful, nearsighted eyes behind the lawyer glasses he had already acquired?

There are never eggshells on the floor or panties on the newspaper shelf. It's not like that.

But her order is superficial.

She's a dreamer. A waffle-baking mother. And a child herself. Every day he sees proof. The worthless plastic rings on his daughters' fingers, won for two kroner from a vending machine. Presents for no reason. The crumpled candy wrappers. The lollipops. Hundreds of chewing gum sticks, gum drops, chocolate bars and licorice laces. All of that disappears into his children's stomachs while the refrigerator is filled to bursting with apples, yoghurt, wholewheat bread and carrots.

Lea's duplicity.

Lea's deceit.

A focal point that makes their previous life into history.

Her high-heeled espadrilles of black silk.

Her dark carpet of hair.

The towels and sheets they wrapped around their bodies.

The juicer and the blender they bought right after Helle's birth.

All those things are in some way a part of the past.

Their laughter is part of the past.

They were sure of one another before they had children.

They were liberated.

Once they saw a pornographic movie together.

They held hands when they walked in.

Lea didn't say anything about the man on her right who suddenly shoved his hand between her thighs. She fought desperately and quietly. Above all she didn't want Dan to notice. If he said anything it would cause a fuss. She pressed her legs together hard.

Dan watched the screen. The woman's pink, over-sized thighs. The man's erection. The skin seemed pink and somehow artificial. Lea thought that actually the hand really didn't do her any harm. That after all it only touched a limited area of her skin. That she should have remembered to put on her long corduroy pants. In a way she had subjected herself to the hand by going into the movie theater. She shouldn't refuse to help a person with something as simple as a sexual need.

They never mentioned the hand.

Otherwise, in contrast to the previous generation, they talked about sex a lot. Of course not when their parents were present. But otherwise.

How? How often? How long? What positions?

When they could hear that the neighbors were home they made love with music playing.

She wondered about his groaning.

He wondered about her closed eyes.

What sort of pictures were being spooled past?

Sometimes at parties Lea got dirt on her stockings from being liberated.

Dan's tongue slid between soft, whiskey-perfumed lips. Teeth cliffs. Tongue fish. The smooth vault of the palate.

Trips to foreign landscapes.

Did they liberate their personal sexuality?

Or did they liberate their sexuality from their persons?

Late at night they returned home together.

Without speaking.

Lea comes toward him with soft, open lips. He pushes her away.

"Sorry," she says.

The children run in the garden. The children's laughter reduces them to silence and freezes their movements.

In the dark their bodies search for one another.

They hold on with teeth, nails, hands, feet. They penetrate through skin. Peck at each other like birds. Scratch like cats.

40

Their bodies are battlefields.

Landscapes for desperate suffering.

They turn heavily away from one another only to reach out for one another again.

The marks on Lea's neck. Are they a sign of love or violence? During the day she covers them with a scarf.

They were a couple. Their first child furnished the apartment with baby clothes and diapers. Lea had never had anything to do with children before. She had never learned how to change a diaper. When she and the baby had been home for two hours all the sheets, hand towels and dish towels they owned, even Dan's handkerchiefs, were wet through.

He ran out and bought crib sheets and absorbent liners with the last of their money.

In the meantime the milk seeped through the blouse that Lea had just received as a gift. And she kept on thinking that the next day she had to figure out how to haul the baby carriage down from the fifth floor and then go back up and get Helle. Then she started crying. And what if she lost the key to the apartment? And what if she didn't lock the door and somebody forced their way in to the child?

But things would get easier. He was almost finished. He already had a job. Of course they had to make payments on his student loans. But still they would be able to save a lot of money. They would buy a house with lots of rooms, a lawn and green, narcotic bubble baths. Helle would take her afternoon nap in the garden and look at leaves and clouds.

The day they bought the house Helle had just turned three. She started digging for ants among the perennials.

The house overwhelmed them.

They knew nothing about the construction of the furnace or any of the electrical installations.

Words like compressor, siphon trap, boiler pressure and photo-cell were foreign to them. As were the shock-like darknesses of the short-circuits and the downpours that penetrated into the house.

The house was like a bewitched forest they had entered unwittingly, only to be trapped by repairs, bills and practical tasks.

Perhaps they were attempting to pacify it when they considered one day, completely seriously, giving it a name.

That was the day they got rid of the Virginia creeper.

He cut through it at the roots. They watched the green leaves wilt and the runners dry up.

"That beautiful creeper—" said the next-door neighbor.

"It was damaging the masonry," said Dan and looked at the newly acquired red-brick wall. The remnants of the plant hanging there traced a net of veins over the wall later and left little ruptures and marks on its surface.

"Maybe we'll plant something else one of these days," he said.

"The creeper attracted so much vermin," said Lea apologetically.

The wall was strikingly naked.

Above the door they discovered a faded patch. There must have been a sign there. "The name of the house," said Lea.

She was five months along and moved heavily on long, sun-tanned legs. She had, more than ever, that Madonna-like quality that made it impossible for him to take his eyes off her.

Lea was full of names. But none of them were applicable to a house. They were names you would give to children, dogs and cats. She admitted their inadequacy.

"Maybe," she said and looked up at the bedroom and the newly furnished children's rooms, "Maybe a sign like that would only make it look like a grave, anyway."

He thought that that was a strange remark for a pregnant woman to make. And that evening they discussed that it would be their life in the house that would give it not one name but thousands and thousands of names.

It's almost remarkable how often they agree with one another. They function as a couple. Or on their own.

He knows when he sits in the train on his way into the city that he is sitting there in order to be able to acquire the things that money can buy. He sits in a non-smoking compartment. He doesn't have a car. He supports public transportation. Also for economic reasons.

The city is aggressive noise and unclean air. A jungle he fights his way through in order to reach his office.

He shuts out the city by closing the white curtains. He switches on the lamp even though it isn't necessary. It's as if the light helps him concentrate. He enjoys the fact that his secretary brings him coffee.

When Lea takes Helle to school she has Malene on the back of the bicycle like a heavy, unmanageable weight.

Helle's knapsack has luminous colors and is big. It catches in the wind.

The wheels of the trucks make them feel frail.

For the time being they're not going to buy a car.

They have enough things. Beautiful new things. Curtains that mustn't be pulled. Chairs that mustn't be climbed in. Woodwork that mustn't get spotted.

Sometimes she finds herself thinking of the experiences they might have had instead. She feels a lack of solidarity with the things they have bought with his money.

"Our money," he says. But she knows that it's his. Because if it had been hers she would have used it for something else. She would have used it up at breakneck speed. She wouldn't have bought things that would last for the rest of her life. She'd rather have worthless rattan furniture, paper cups, thin soft fabrics, excursions and trips.

43

Things wear her down. Things put a harness on Malene's energy, or she puts a harness on it, dutifully, because of the things.

Sometimes she feels it's all his fault.

He invented staircases and walls. And Malene's fingers on the walls. He invented spiders, the vacuum cleaner, rings around the bathtub and the plugged-up drain.

She knows she's being unfair. But she takes revenge anyway. She puts the crystal glasses in the dishwasher and never kills moths.

On weekends she wishes she were somewhere else.

But he prefers a cozy family life, slippers, old clothes and newspapers.

He is recluctant to go out. But enjoys bringing people home.

With her yielding gestures and her apologetic smile, Lea is the perfect hostess.

She can make a meal which was carefully planned seem simple and everyday. Something that arose spontaneously, maybe because of the weather.

She makes sure that there are pretzels, dog biscuits and home-made ice cream waffles in the house.

Sometimes he catches himself feeling as though he were a guest himself.

One evening he saw her stack the thin, white plates in the dishwasher using precisely the same tired, sullen gesture that she used to toss things into the garbage pail.

They didn't break.

He walks across the grass. It bends under the soles of his shoes. It's been a long time since he has walked in the grass at just this spot.

He should have shouted something. Flushed them up like birds.

He hears footsteps in the house.

Maybe she's packing a suitcase.

Maybe she'll walk through the garden in a minute, wearing black and standing straight with her luggage in her hand.

Or in the thin, white suit and the high-heeled shoes that sink down into the grass a bit.

He goes in.

She isn't in the living room or the bedroom.

For an instant he really believes that she has disappeared and he assumes that what he feels is relief. She is standing in the bathroom brushing her hair. The white spot at her temple has spread like a pale, star-shaped wound. The wrinkles under her eyes have become sharper, or else it's because of the light. Her back is naked and beautiful.

She looks at him the way she did when she was very young and went to the movies to fall in love. As though she were, at this moment, high on some feeling. Or perhaps it's just a little, dull ember which will quickly burn out.

She moves slowly, with a conscious sensuality he hasn't noticed before.

"When," he thinks, "do two bodies have the same feeling in the same room?"

Waiting

"—Well—" says the doctor.

He pulls the rubber liner off his finger and throws it away.

She lifts her legs out of the iron stirrups.

She didn't take the time to put her clothes on the stool. They're lying in a pile on the floor. Her panty-hose hang from her fingers.

"Here you are." He sticks a paper towel in behind the curtain to her.

She dries herself dutifully and since there isn't a wastepaper basket nearby she rolls up the paper towel and hides it in the bottom of her handbag. The tips of her fingers brush the piece of paper on which she has written down everything she should remember to ask about. She just doesn't have the energy to lace up her shoes.

She stands in front of the desk with her bag in her hand.

The thin, brown hair on his forehead rests on the edge of his glasses. On the crown of his head there's a little bald spot. She feels like touching it with her forefinger or tapping it. The thought embarasses her. She looks away from him. Up at a poster about how healthy vitamins and vegetables will make you.

Maybe that's what she lacks. Fruit, vitamins and vegetables. No. But it would be easier for her to ask what's wrong if her body were well-preserved and smooth. "Nonsense—" she thinks, "as if a doctor weren't familiar with bodies in decay. Bodies with crooked toenails, calluses, varicose veins and bunions."

"Do you think it's anything serious?"

But her voice is jumpy and thin, as if the question just forced its

47

way out of the handbag.

"I don't think so—we can't tell for sure until you've been thoroughly examined."

He seems optimistic and healthy.

"It may be a few weeks before we can get you into the hospital. —Take care," he says and presses her hand.

"Thank you. The same to you—"

He starts as if "same to you" were improper and might hint at something frail in him. But he keeps on smiling.

She bends her head and walks quickly through the waiting room. It seems as though the people who are waiting look right through her clothes.

Outside she breathes a sigh of relief. It's only ten o'clock and the city seems cool and clean like a newly-swept factory or a machine that's just been overhauled. She quickens her pace and notices that she's put her panty-hose on wrong.

At this time of day she's usually sitting at the cash register in her deep-green smock, watching the groceries come gliding past to be rung up. Someone must have taken her place. Maybe Bente, Annette or Tove. She imagines them, the way they arrive in the morning and sleepily pull on their smocks. For a moment she feels a sudden tenderness towards them. She feels like buying pastry and treating everyone at coffee break.

But they said themselves that she should take the day off. They practically forced her to make an appointment with the doctor because she fainted into a stack of tomato cans.

If she shows up they'll start asking questions and being suitably concerned and suitably comforting and they'll say that nothing's wrong and she should just take it easy and relax. She wouldn't be able to stand it. All that common sense. And their promises to visit.

She digs her heels into the cobblestones. In a way it's their fault.

It's because of them she's going to be hospitalized. Now they can sit around and talk about her condition and collect money for flowers. As though fainting spells weren't a human right.

But she could have fooled them. She could have talked about her insomnia instead. Then she never would have been exposed.

Because that's what happened. Her feelings have been exposed. A little irregularity, something that might be a symptom of a tumor. And now she's suddenly exposed as unhealthy.

If she goes home now she won't be able to stop thinking. But what if she goes over to Hanne's. If she tells her only sister what she thinks is wrong. Maybe Hanne could convince her not to believe it.

Suddenly she misses her. Hanne, who inherited their father's ease. Hanne's careless generosity with film tickets, picture post cards and expensive Sunday pastries. Their mother was ambitious and imaginative. That's why there were always too many ruffles on their dresses. Even their underwear was imaginative, knit with angora yarn in complicated lace patterns as though that could hide the fact that their father was usually unemployed.

He always left home in the morning and returned late in the afternoon. Sometimes he was very cheerful and there was a sweet smell of cherry wine streaming around him. "Here comes the top dog," he sang.

On the day they had to tell the teacher their father's profession, she said he was a top executive. But nobody would believe it.

When she's sitting on the train she regrets not calling first. But now it's too late. In stolen glances she sees women behind the hedges. The elderly ones, the very young ones, and the ones who are her age. They're equipped with garden shears and hats. Some of them have small, downy children who yell in wading pools. They skin their knees and let themselves be comforted with cheap ice cream.

The noise from the fifteen camel bells at Hanne's door seems to spread itself around the house more than it penetrates into it. And only after she rattles the letter slit does Mick open the door and gaze at her with his five-year-old deep and cynical look.

"Do you have anything with you?" he asks.

Ashamed of her thoughtlessness she searches in her billfold.

"That's not exactly what I had in mind," he says sadly and looks at the five kroner.

She feels the softness of the carpets and at the same time the word "hall" runs through her mind and as usual makes her feel self-conscious.

Hanne comes down from upstairs with a hair dryer in hand and the cord dangling behind her.

"Lily," she says, "My goodness—I didn't know."

She pushes some orange, pink and purple knitting off the sofa.

"Lily", the name she doesn't like, sounds like a shout in the sink —and Hanne fills the kettle from the tap and counts instant coffee in spoonfuls. As though Hanne, too, moves in the periphery of her name and her being. As though her shyness and her fear are contagious.

The cigarette is a white antenna in Hanne's gentle face.

"Are you on vacation or do you have the day off?"

"I've been to the doctor's.—I'm going to be hospitalized for some tests—"

"If only it were me."

"What do you mean by that?"

"Nothing.—Just lie there and be waited on.—Everything you suddenly don't have to deal with.—Pretty soon the three day-care children will be here. And my hair isn't even dry."

A fleeting worry passes over Hanne's face. Then the camel bells ring. She gets up and smiles eagerly to a young, corduroy-clad girl who turns three children loose in the room. They immediately dash over to the bowl with cookies.

"Hey," says Mick who comes into the room at that moment. "How come I don't get a treat?"

"There's a bag for you out on the drainboard."

The corduroy girl disappears as suddenly as she appeared.

Hanne looks as though she might be considering going out into the kitchen and undertaking the task of dividing the cookies among the children fairly. But the children are already out there.

"Kids—" she mumbles and sits down.

"Do you remember," says Lily, "the time we had a fight with the potted plants?"

"Yes. What makes you think of that now?"

"No reason.—I've got to go."

"But—I was just going to fix lunch. At least stay and eat. And wait and say hello to Torben."

But she's already gotten up.

Suddenly she realizes that the day should be spent doing all the things that need doing before she's hospitalized.

Her housecoat ought to be clean. Her overnight bag ought to be packed. She needs to buy a new pair of slippers. A new toothbrush.

She looks at her watch in panic. "There's so much I have to do."

"Well you have to eat no matter what."

She has to be completely ready. Maybe an empty, flat bed will suddenly appear. Maybe she will receive notice in the morning mail that her body, and nobody else's is going to be admitted and placed in that exact bed.

The words trip over one another as she attempts to explain. Hanne looks a little insulted or maybe just surprised. But she can't let that worry her. She runs all the way to the station. Contrary to her expectations she makes the train. She breathes a sigh of relief when she puts the key in the lock.

She sits down on the sofa for a minute without taking off her coat.

But she can't settle down. It's as though little capsules of energy were being released in her. She has to get everything done.

The cloth loop breaks when she pulls the housecoat down from the hook and stuffs it into a plastic bag together with some underwear and handkerchiefs. And luckily she makes it to the laundromat before all the machines are taken. She forgets to hold a cup under the spout when she gets her soap. The powder shoots out and settles like snow on the floor and on her shoes. She scrapes it up. Along with a little dust. But she can't let all that soap lie on the floor and since the clothing isn't very dirty it will undoubtedly be cleaned, anyway.

From a black plastic chair she follows the housecoat's travels. The long stay in the washing machine. The wet bundle she presses into the centrifuge. And finally the dryer where she watches it spread itself out and descend through the air—soft, falling, free. She'll have to sew the rip in the neck.

At home she breaks two eggs into a pan and finds the sewing box. When the loop has been repaired she finds a hole in one of the pockets. She is astonished by her presence of mind when she turns off the eggs.

Stockings, handkerchiefs, underwear. And she might as well get the right skirt and the right blouse ready. The skirt needs to be ironed and her shoes need to be polished one more time. She stands up and eats cold fried eggs.

Suddenly it's past four o'clock and it's too late to buy slippers. She has to have something to read, too. And maybe some knitting. And a pen and some cards. The sofa is already covered with her things. The hospitalization won't fit into her overnight bag.

And the plants. The plants that cover her window with their dark-green leaves and their pale, rangy shoots. Shut-in, they grow in spite of aphids and too much or too little water. It would be easiest to throw them out. Otherwise she could give somebody her key. She listens at the door. Then she carefully takes the big royal ivy down. She listens again, then she carries it out and with closed eyes tosses it down the garbage chute. The other plants aren't as heavy.

Afterwards the window stares at her. Bright, naked and raw. She closes the curtains and starts taking food out of the refrigerator in order to defrost it. She uncorks the white wine since she can't keep it cold anymore, anyway. When she's drunk three glasses her movements become heavy and rolling.

"You have alcohol in your bloodstream, Miss Lily Jensen," she mumbles as she bends over the sink and pours shampoo on her dry hair. "Hell," she thinks as she rinses it out, "I'll just wash it three times instead of twice."

But standing bent over makes her dizzy. Resolute, she fills the bathtup halfway and sits down in it. The shower sprays on her head. She feels effective and practical and when her hair is rinsed she leans back and relaxes, until gurgling in her ear and the taste of shampoo in her mouth wake her up. The bath water has run out into the hallway. She sighs absentmindedly at the thought that now she has to dry both the floor and herself. She uses the same little bathtowel for both tasks and drinks the rest of the wine to get rid of the soap taste. When she turns off the light in the bedroom there's a little twinge in her heart and otherwise just soft, quivering darkness.

Maybe the ticking of the clock wakes her up. Little metallic drops that fall through the darkness and are sprinkled uselessly over her body.

She doesn't want to hear it.

She stretches so that her joints creak. And reaches out anyway for the alarm clock with its green, luminous numbers. Alive in the dark like cat's eyes. Three-thirty as usual.

She rolls over and tries to relax. Now her wristwatch is too close to her ear. An infant, insect-like ticking fills her head with little, tiny swarming noises.

Her arm is asleep. Her head is awake. And she's sweating.

She's tired. Tired to the bone. Her muscles are hard and heavy. They clench themselves against the pillow, which she shakes and pushes and shakes.

But it's not fair. There's no reason to be nervous. She's always done her job. Her cash register balances.

She shouldn't have let the doctor write.

She should just have asked for some pills to cure her of insomnia and sweat. And to cure her of this fatigue deep in her bones.

If she could stop thinking. Stop being tense. Just stop.

During the day it's not so bad. But she has to sleep to be able to take it. Sleep to be able to get up.

Little by little it feels as though she is freed from the cramp-like hold of her muscles—as though she is nothing but the weight of her skinny bones which falls backwards into darkness—gone.

She's walking over a gleaming, icebound lake. She's searching for something without knowing exactly what it is. She pulls her heavy legs over the ice and walks stooped forward and slowly. The cold penetrates into her. But she keeps on walking until she reaches the place. He is lying under the ice which has formed an air bubble around him. His glossy red jacket shines through. When she bends over and stretches her arm out, he's gone. And she loses her footing and falls backwards. Falls and falls through huge, vaulted rooms. She hits bottom with a jerk.

The bed is shaking. She's wide-awake. And not even ten minutes have passed. For no reason she's had the usual dream.

He came and went so quickly that there's no reason for her to search for him in her sleep.

She's hardly entitled to call him a lover. He was a passer-by whose hands stroked her sandy-colored hair so that she thought about dyeing it red or having it streaked.

She also bought a new sofa and beer and sherry and a rabbit fur.

She didn't protect herself when she slept with him, out of ignorance, perhaps, or shyness. Or maybe she wanted a child.

She had sweated then, too. But there wasn't this stale and bitter smell. There wasn't this heaviness in her body.

Maybe he does his shopping somewhere else now because of her.

Hopefully that will be the first and last time that she is to blame for a drop in sales.

He didn't buy much. The afternoon newspapers. Cigarettes. Beer. Once in a while a little fruit.

One day he pushed his cart into her heel by accident while she was standing and pricing goods. The little gasp she uttered could just as well have been from surprise as from pain.

He said he was sorry and asked if it hurt.

She shook her head. On her way home her foot swelled up and the next day she limped a bit. But nobody noticed it.

He was thirty-two and divorced. Sometimes there was a searching, awkward look in his eyes which totally did away with the arrogance that might have frightened her otherwise.

She had just turned thirty-six but for the last ten years had looked like she was around thirty. Once in a while she had tried to accentuate her personality by using cosmetics. But the make-up made her small, regular features and light-blue eyes so doll-like that after a few days she returned to her usual pale, anonymous condition.

She noticed that he always turned to the pages with horse races while he waited at the register. He almost always wore a short, red flight jacket. And sometimes he had his trouser legs tucked into tall rubber boots. Because of that she thought he went riding and to be on the safe side she learned the names of the horses, the trainers and the jockeys by heart. Sometimes she felt as though she were lifted up into an elegant, risky atmosphere by reading the distinguished foreign names.

The day he invited her to the derby she bought new shoes of delicate suede and considered putting a rose in the belt of her porcelain blue silk dress. But when she entered the spectators' stand she was glad she hadn't done it. If there was anything having to do with elegance and big hats, it took place somewhere else. But it must have been there because she saw it the next day in the newspaper.

But already during the first race it started raining right where she was standing. He was wearing his usual red jacket and didn't notice it. He was betting together with a little man who had prune-colored eyes and was wearing a bicycle seat cover pulled down over his forehead, evidently as protection against the rain.

They carried on a matter-of-fact discussion about the horses and their chances on the slippery track.

At every race they insisted that she hold the coupons because she probably had the most luck.

She shook her head and held on tight.

In three of the races she bet ten crowns herself, elated and shocked at her frivolity.

"Unlucky at gambling, lucky in love," she thought when they were sitting in the train without having won a thing.

Later he went home with her.

He called her apartment a doll house and was touched by her pale body and meager sexual experience.

In the morning she toasted rolls, poured juice and made coffee.

He visited her five times in all.

Each time she set the table in the living room with flowers and candles and stood with glowing cheeks at the electric range to produce intimate dishes.

She should have made it easier on herself. Just have opened some cans and not have herded him into the living room with a glass of sherry or a beer. Probably he thought that setting the table for two courses was too middle class. And she didn't even dare ask if she might darn the hole in his sweater.

Suddenly the alarm clock rings. And she must have slept anyway because she is so confused that she knocks it over when she turns it off.

She pulls on an old trench coat so that the housecoat won't get dirty. The floor in the bathroom is still wet and the towel is lying in the hallway.

As soon as she has washed herself the sweat is there again. In spite of cold water, clean clothes and eau de cologne. The neighbor is listening to the radio. A high bright voice singing something from an opera penetrates through the wall and into her like a scream cutting through her body.

In the living room she sits down and looks out the window, over to the piles of clothes on the sofa, and back again.

As soon as the mail arrives she'll phone and ask for a week's vacation.

She opens the door to the hallway so that she can keep an eye on the letter slit. Luckily only an advertisement for furniture drops in. She leafs through it three times to make sure there's nothing hidden in it. Then she pulls herself together and calls the management.

"Is there anything wrong?"

"No." She hurries to say good-bye.

First she'll make a list of everything she's missing. Then she'll go to the bank and then go shopping. When she's packed everything into the overnight bag she's planning on buying for the occasion she'll feel calm.

She fixes herself up with great care and even puts a little old rouge on her cheeks so that she'll look healthy.

To her own surprise she's in high spirits when she finds the right overnight bag. She buys a frozen pizza to take home and warms it in the oven while she carefully places all the newly acquired items in the bag. She folds the housecoat and puts it on top. There's plenty of room and later on she can use the bag when she travels.

She drinks a glass of red wine along with the pizza and falls asleep. The telephone wakes her up. Hanne asks her over for dinner. But she's too tired. That evening she watches all the television programs glide past like a shadow landscape with changing voices. During the night she tiptoes out a number of times to check in front of the letter slit. Each time she staggers relieved back to the bedroom. It doesn't matter if she has insomnia, she doesn't have to get up for a whole week. After the mailman has passed by she sleeps soundly.

She wakes up at noon and remembers that it's Saturday. She pulls on some clothes and just manages to shop at the nearest grocery store before it closes.

In the afternoon she pulls herself together and takes a walk. Not towards the center of the city but towards the outskirts, where it seems to her that the air should be fresh.

She sticks her hands deep in the pockets of the rabbit fur coat. It's a little too warm. But she wants to use it. She strides throught the park. There are still flowers. Roses that won't let their leaves be worn away. Buds that are rotting because of the moisture. And dark, bitter-smelling chrysanthemums. The colors seem unbecoming and damp. She thinks about snow. Graphically black and white and the sharp, blue air.

Outside the park there's a gravestone dealer.

The gravestones stand in nice, even rows. A white one, a grey one, a black one, a pink one and one with brown stripes. If she had to choose would she take natural stone or one with pious, white doves? They are all still naked. They're waiting, like an empty room—like unused linen—like dogs without masters. Waiting for a name—dignity— friendship.

Suddenly she discovers that she's standing there smiling. If anybody saw her they'd think she was crazy. If anyone was there choosing a gravestone in earnest they'd be hurt by her smile.

At home she looks in the mirror.

"I'm afraid," she thinks, "afraid of going crazy. Or maybe I'm more afraid that someone might discover it. I'm afraid people won't like me because I act wrong. I try to appear friendly and relaxed. But suddenly there's a trembling under my skin as though all the muscles were being tensed so that they can break through. If anyone notices that they'll realize I'm pretending."

On Sunday she won't go out at all. Better to stay in bed and read the newspaper and sleep.

After breakfast she reads the personals. Serious, positive, unhappy, sexy. All sorts of longings and loneliness in alphabetical order. She wonders if he might be one of them. Maybe he would write to her via a newspaper. But he has her address.

Around two the telephone rings. And when it's rung a couple of times she pulls out the plug and reads the advertisements once more, moving from love to assorted. Sectional kitchens, window moldings, dentures and an herbal doctor. At first she lets her eyes glide on. Then it strikes her that this just might be her slavation. If she gets well she won't have to be hospitalized. She decides herself.

She gets up and cuts out the advertisement and puts it in her billfold. Suddenly she feels calm. She makes coffee and sits down to do some knitting on the white winter top and everything is so secure and quiet and Sunday-like that the white knit stitches slip easily and boringly from needle to needle. And calm and boredom purr in her like a cat. It continues until the doorbell rings.

She sits completely still, terrified that the clicking of the needles might give her away. The bell rings twice, then the steps disappear resignedly down the stairs and nothing has been stuck in through the letter slit. She spends most of the rest of the day in the bedroom and listens for a long time before allowing herself to use the toilet.

The next morning before the mail arrives she calls a taxi to drive her to the herbal doctor's address. When she opens the door there are ten wilted pink roses on her doormat. She tosses them into the chute without slowing down. And her voice is quite ordinary and clear when she tells the driver the address.

In the old man's room her fear vanishes. His eyes are as bright and alive as a child's. His skin is wrinkled and brown, as though he's out in the sun a lot.

On a bookcase in back of him are bags and jars with dried plants.

He looks at her eyes and hands. His own hands are firm and warm and he touches her as though she were a child or a beloved animal.

She doesn't think to ask what's wrong with her when he gives her the bag with miracle tea. If she drinks a liter every day and takes long walks the air, the tea and the exercise will make it go away.

She starts that day, after having phoned and gotten her vacation extended.

She drinks the tea in large, bitter gulps while she thinks about his friendliness and about the fact that now she'll escape.

She walks and the earth is a pain under her feet. She gives birth to rays of pain that flow out of her body and make her warm and sweaty. The only thing she's afraid of is fainting on the street. Every day she sweeps the mail into a corner.

The day she meets him, still wearing his red flight jacket his pants stuffed into his rubber boots, she has stopped dreaming at night and during the day.

He is very far away. It's as though she has to exert herself to see him through a massive fatigue.

She doesn't understand his embarrassment and his explanations that he tried to write to her and that he moved back for the boy's sake but it didn't work out anyway.

"But time heals all wounds," he finishes up heroically.

"Maybe not all of them," she mumbles, beginning to speak.

"You have to let yourself be hospitalized," he says, "it's the only sensible thing."

She doesn't know if it's common sense that propels her, the next day, through the gate and into the passages between the low pavilions. She's looking for a sign that says "Admissions". She notes with satisfaction that there aren't any more leaves on the trees. And he is carrying her overnight bag.

Separate Ways

We go down the stairs. I hold the door open for her.

Outside the wind makes the big straw hat with the artificial rose bob. As if it were floating on water.

The pain becomes small and sharp and somehow detached from me.

People are eating hot dogs in the square. The pigeons fly up. We turn toward one another, detached from one another.

"Bye," she says, as though we had agreed just to say "bye".

She chooses one direction. I have to choose the opposite.

A young man offers me God as a comic book. I give him five kroner and put God in my pocket. "God loves you," he says and smiles.

Young people are wearing thin T-shirts with Tarzan, Tordenskjold, racing cars, purebred horses, moon rockets and Marilyn Monroe printed on light cotton over their hearts, over their pulses and breasts. And otherwise these blue, ragged colors. Cowboys. Summer clouds. Water.

I'm thirty-two. And not really young any more.

Ragged clouds. That's what it was like that day, too.

We went up the stairs. Girls wore high, thin heels then. You could always hear her footsteps. Our clothing was so new that it sort of crackled around us. We were nervous.

We sat in the waiting room together with a foreigner and a thin, blond woman. The woman was older than him. He kept on squeezing her hands. How much did they know about one another?

Later a gaunt man wearing glasses that were crooked read a

passage out loud for us. We didn't grasp the words. But we said yes in the right places, anyway, in high, clear voices. We did it passionately, as though we were about to commit a crime or something holy.

All that time there must have been people outside, gazing indifferently at the town hall and the fountain while they ate boiled hot dogs and grilled hot dogs with coarse, brown skin. Or perhaps they crumbled a bit of the warm bread for the pigeons and let them sit on their hands. People did that then, too.

Later our families threw rice at us. We drove away in a car with a tail of tin cans. We were married.

How old-fashioned we were then—twelve years ago. We could have been our own parents.

We were stable. We had office jobs. I had saved a little money. She collected silver teaspoons. But we got married primarily because of the apartment. We were lucky. Falling in love coincided with a two-room apartment with kitchen and bath. Others who were just as in love had to take the streetcar every night.

In the beginning being newly-wed absorbed us. We furnished the apartment as comfortably as we could. She made lamp shades out of straw. And we bought a big mirror so that we could be sure we looked presentable when we left.

We all looked presentable then. Short hair. Clothing neatly pressed and nice. Her hair flipped out in curls at her ears. And she felt sick if there was a run in her stockings.

Her thin smooth stockings and her lips. That was important. She had lipstick in gold-colored tubes. She filled in her lips, made them full, smooth, damp, sensual. Ginger-pink. Orange-flower. She stood in her slip while she did it. In the beginning we couldn't afford housecoats.

But as soon as we had money we started buying. We loved buying. Clothing. Furniture. Even jewelry. We were sensuous consumers. The supermarkets and the department stores made us feel exhilarated even when we had just a little bit of money in our billfolds. Toward the end of the month we were almost always depressed. And we always had a bill at the dairy store.

Maybe we were bored. Sometimes I think we were bored.

Later everything started happening fast. It was as though everything that was fashionable happened in jumps. Take rock music for example. We didn't have time to get tired of one group before another one was more famous. And I didn't manage to figure out where to buy hash before it was so ordinary that you might as well not bother. And as for sex, we only learned a few positions and looked at a couple of magazines. Then even pornography was worn out. And the latest thing was love and intercourse lying on your side.

Then came the women's movement. The third world. And pollution.

It was all fashionable in some way. And we did what we could to identify ourselves with our roles. But we were amateurs and sometimes the roles were difficult to learn. Maybe we didn't develop because new trends kept coming all the time. New roles. And we were afraid of being too slow. Afraid of not being with it.

I don't remember those years as anything continuous. More like a series of pictures. Some of them over-exposed, some soft and secretive as in old films.

It's all quite ordinary. Quite normal. And fashionable sometimes.

Divorce is ordinary, too. But I feel as though it's not really fashionable.

Maybe it's more appropriate for her.

She wants to find herself, she says. Take stock of herself. What does she mean by that? Was she lost all that time? Or is she going to hold a rummage sale?

In the beginning she didn't know phrases like that. In the beginning she was very sweet-tempered. Or perhaps insecure would be more correct. She was always worried about not being fine enough. Capable enough. Attractive enough. Any attentiveness or flirtation flattered her. Even if it was some random, half-drunken fellow or the Italian deck chair hand who was bald, squat and hairy all over his body.

It wasn't because she had a large sexual appetite that her eyes and her posture always said, "Do you like me?" Actually she didn't like sex very much. Not even when it was fashionable. It was as if it always had to be a debt or an ache. Still, she was capable of being kittenishly affectionate and her moaning sounded like a summons or a prayer. She could let herself be obliterated in a remarkably gentle way. But sometimes she did it out of politeness or just so that you would like her. And she was enormously relieved when she read in a magazine one day that it wasn't her fault, and most certainly didn't have anything to do with her performance, that she didn't experience orgasm.

Maybe the arrival of the women's movement was good for her. It took her a long time to pick it up. That was one of the roles that was hardest for her to identify with, I think. But she did it.

It confused me, suddenly being sent down to the laundromat. Or when she held long, energetic lectures about her reasonable demands. She said, among other things, that I should hang my clothes up myself and that I wasn't to wipe my shoes off with a handkerchief if I saw a speck of dust on them right as I was going out the door. I started wiping them off on my trouser leg instead and I took my clothes to the dry cleaners myself.

She started talking about her breasts as though they were two independent and unpleasant creatures.

Up until then she had paid a lot of attention to them. She bought lace-trimmed bras and did special exercises so that her breasts wouldn't disappear during a diet or start to hang before she was forty. Now there were no limits to how badly they were to be treated, those breasts. Precisely her shape expressed the typical middle-class dream. They

66

were useless. They were out of step with the times.

If you wanted to have breasts at all you could buy some. Or have your own blown up like balloons. You might even get some help from the national health insurance.

One evening she burned the lace-trimmeds. She started buying her underwear in a men's clothing store.

Then the baby arrived.

That is to say, she got pregnant between the women's movement and pollution. And she wasn't suited to it.

I don't know why I kept on expecting the Mona-Lisa-smile, the calm and the knitting that would grow between her fingers.

She threw up.

Her breasts took revenge. They swelled up. Sofia Loren. Anita Ekberg. They couldn't compare with her. Her breasts broke all the records for sex and middle-class dreams.

Relaxation was in. She took a course to learn how to relax and sigh. I never heard her sigh. She swept through pregnancy in wide office dresses, gritting her teeth, bitching like a fishwife and swearing like a sailor.

It didn't give her hope or tranquillity. But rather a sharp, outward-directed anger.

Her body wasn't suited to it, either.

After the birth she was sick. She lay all alone in a white room and cried because it was a girl. I tried to comfort her by saying that if everything continued at this rate it would be best to be a girl in twenty years. But she kept on crying and said that surely I could realize it was something physiological. And even if the baby ever got to be twenty at all, with our dirty air, there probably wouldn't be any water or meat, anyway. And if there were anything edible and drinkable left over, then all the colored peoples, whom we had oppressed and were still oppressing, would have the right to come and eat and drink it all away from our child.

She felt guilty about having given birth to this white, defenseless creature which belonged to a decadent race that was dying out. A child that would demand clean, soft things. Bubble baths. Sub-development lawns, her own room and bed. In Asia the little children didn't have to clean their plates. In India you could get a transistor radio for letting yourself be sterilized. Or you could be forced to. In some countries they printed gaudy patterns of IUDs and birth control pills on soft cotton.

It was as if she wished she had given birth to the baby in a hut made of palm leaves or on the street in Bombay. Then at least the only way things could go was up.

I went out to look at the baby. I tried to smile. But this new and antiseptic creature, motionless and wrinkled, was like a shock. It was like seeing one's first corpse. I was incapable of imagining that this creature would ever have problems that resembled ours.

She and the baby came home. She nursed and bottle-fed. The women's movement and pollution continued. And the baby continued. The baby lost its dark hair and grew fine, fair hair. The baby learned to turn its head. To crawl and eat mashed food.

Karina—that was the name she was given—was the first thing in our existence that wasn't somehow abstract.

We felt that it was our duty to make her happy, package her in happiness, vaccinate her with it, since we, after all, had so thoughtlessly brought her into this doubtful world on a planet where we had, bit by bit, picked and eaten everything. There would only be a few measly left-overs and all our trash and dirt left for her. But no tigers, elephants or butterflies.

We changed her disposable diapers and felt deeply depressed by the thought that one day she would climb mountains of eternally shredded plastic.

Once in a while we looked at ourselves in the big mirror. We had changed.

We weren't young, sensuous consumers any more. At any rate our consumption didn't have the same greedy, primitive joy any more.

Our hair had grown longer. Especially hers. But we hadn't grown old. We had reached the age where one has almost forgotten childhood, puberty and all the terrible things you have to go through before you turn your face forward and become definitively unhappy.

But none of us look noticeably older. We get wrinkles. Our hair gets thinner. And our bodies less perfect. But at the same time we reduce our demands for perfection. And our clothing becomes more youthful, more carefree, more casual. These young, blue, washed-out colors. As innocent as children's overalls. We borrow clothes. We dress up. We're yachtsmen without boats. Peasants without grain. And cowboys without horses.

But still. Somehow or other we were locked in. She became a housewife and was depressed about being a housewife. And I realized that I would never earn enough money for anything other than the two-room apartment we had married into.

She was almost always irritable and tired.

Sometimes we went to the movies separately. Sometimes our friends visited us. And Karina woke up and screamed as though she were possessed. On Sundays we took her to the zoo and showed her the elephants and all the beasts of prey that were dying out. But she liked the sparrows best.

We drifted apart.

For a while I had an affair with another woman. She was young and silent. Perhaps there would only have been pollution and the women's movement and who knows what else if she had opened her mouth. I wasn't particularly interested in her doing that.

Of course she found out and said that actually she didn't care. She couldn't be provoked in that way at all, she said. She was tired. Tired, that's what she was most of all.

Only when the family visited—her family, Karina's family—did she insist on creating the illusion that we were happy. She played tender scenes from a little happy family's life.

In her opinion her mother, father, brother, sisters, uncles, aunts and cousins had enough problems. And for their sake she took on the role of happy young mother and happy young housewife.

At times I almost believe she rehearsed these scenes which irritated me with their false and superficial tranquillity. She promised Karina chocolate and ice cream for cooperating. She made much less of an effort for my family.

If one of her Sundays failed she could be depressed for weeks. If Karina was impossible. If I complained. Or if we argued. If she felt that she had been cheated out of her sham idyll it was in fact almost certain that we would start arguing.

Sometimes I thought that our arguments resembled something from Bergman movies. At other times they didn't rise above the level of comic strips. And it was only for economic reasons that cups and saucers didn't fly through the air.

It must have been after one of those failed Sundays that I went to the bathroom. She hadn't locked the door and I didn't know she was there.

Her arms were resting on the edge of the sink. In her right hand she held a razor blade. She was gazing into the mirror with an almost infatuated look. As though she wanted to hypnotize herself into making use of the blade which rested between her fingers. Smooth, sharp and luminous.

Was she serious? Would she really have done it? Or was she just playing? Was she trying to make her stay in the bathroom more exciting by doing that?

When she saw me she hid it.

She said, "I didn't hear you."

I said, "It's going to rain soon."

When we were in bed she reached out her hand to me. Ordinarily she never did that.

That summer we rented a house at the beach.

We took it easier with Karina. She was two years old now. And her body was so round that it looked like it was rolling over the lawn. We didn't try so hard any more to stuff her with nourishing food. She preferred vanilla ice cream and dirt.

We tried to grow close to one another again, with our beings and with our sunburnt bodies.

It was a kind of agreement. We had to avoid divorce for Karina's sake. We also ate meatballs and ice cream for her sake. And we spent hours at the beach.

But we had drifted apart. We were astonished by each other's skin. We were astonished by each other's movements. Teeth. Hair. But there was no delight in the astonishment.

One day I saw her sunbathing naked on the fenced-in terrace. It didn't suit her. There was nothing frank about her nakedness. She had combed her hair straight back so that it wouldn't get in the way of an even tan. She lay with one arm under her head and with her face turned towards the light. Her hips had gotten broad. She bent her knees slightly. And her resting, lightly-golden figure reminded me of the little antique ivory statues doctors once used with modest women.

I imagined the closed rooms and the long-skirted women wearing violet and lavender-blue veils.

And when I touched her warm, dry skin in the dark and she received me patiently, I seemed to hear, constantly, a small intimate voice, "Doctor, this is where it hurts."

We moved back to town and kept on arguing. It was somehow inevitable. We drifted apart or were pushed apart: She, Karina and I.

71

Once in a while we discussed things in a polite and level-headed manner while smoking cigarettes. Once in a while we felt united. It was like a wound we had to blow on all the time. Or tear open.

There was still the dream of being able to make contact through skin. Through sweat. Through these movements at once heavy and acrobatic. An itch or an ache which releases desire or irritation. This moaning and sighing. "Ah", says the tongue. "Beloved", says the tongue. "God", says the tongue to this salty mass of flesh. To feel united again. To be loved. Be something. Because of the dream of unattainable happiness. Or because of a wish to be scratched in inaccessible places.

But she didn't need that anymore, she said. She didn't need the smell of sex anymore or the boring into her flesh.

She said that even before our lawyers began writing to one another and showing us the letters. And before I met her at their offices wearing clothes I didn't recognize.

She doesn't plan to marry again. Otherwise she's full of plans. She seems so sure of herself when I run into her now and again. When we go down a random staircase and she says "Hi".

Her nose seems stubborn under the romantic hat. She's put spurs on her boots. What does that mean? A flower. A spur. It vanishes. Ten years ago they always went to bed with each other in the films. Now they box.

We vanish. She, Karina and I. Like a series of pictures, fleeting and not particularly coherent. Did love also exist somewhere in those pictures? And why doesn't one indicate it in some way when it vanishes?

We go our separate ways now. Or we run away.

The pain is quite small and sharp and somehow detached from me.

When I meet my friends, or our friends, there's a shadow between us. As though they were afraid I might start talking about it.

We turn away from one another. Detached from one another.

72

We don't scream. We don't hate. That kind of thing isn't done in our generation. We're level-headed. We're carefree.

She chooses one direction. I have to choose the opposite.

Maybe this is temporary, too. A kind of role. In any event it's ordinary.

The Stronger II

"The Stronger II" is an attempt to write a paraphrase of "The Stronger" by August Strindberg. The idea is Pernille Grumme's.

A cafe with small round marble tables and mirrors. It's the afternoon of December 24th. Anne is sitting at a table. She pats her hair, sips the cup of Irish coffee which stands on the table in front of her. There's also a newspaper on the table but she doesn't look at it. At the moment she is preoccupied with her shopping list. She crosses out and checks off. She glances down into the bags which are placed around the chair. Once in a while she appears to doubt whether she really has remembered everything. The bags contain fruit, candy, toys and many packages of perfume.

Beth enters. She is dressed expensively and with personal flair. She moves confidently and freely. She has a little purse and is carrying a shopping bag. When she sees Anne, she stops. At first she doesn't know, perhaps, whether she should greet Anne or find a table farther away. But she makes up her mind quickly.

Beth: My goodness—it's you—Have you got time to sit here?—I really didn't think that you went out alone.

Anne looks up. Her nod is friendly but a little shy.

Beth: (glances at the bags) Look at what you're lugging around—Yes—

75

it's demanding—Don't you have two children now—No *three.*

Anne nods affirmingly and smiles a bit at the three.

The waitress brings a glass of Scotch for Beth. She takes a couple of fast gulps.

Beth: My goodness—don't you remember—I told you then, too—You shouldn't marry so young and certainly not somebody who was so much more experienced than you—"At least try living together first" I said—But there you were, a white bride, two weeks later— And now you have three children.

Anne looks around, as if she were a little worried that others might overhear what is being said. Then she bends over her list.

Beth: *(impulsively)* Look—Just look and see the present I bought for myself—*(she takes a pair of long, beautiful boots out of the bag. She caresses them and puts her hands into them)*
Aren't they gorgeous—And so so soft—Sometimes I think there's something almost sensual about leather—*(thoughtfully)* Of course—Bob didn't much care for it—Boots—far too masculine.

Anne looks down at her legs. She's wearing stockings and shoes.

Beth: *(continues, carefree)* But then I don't have to think about that anymore—his need for stockings and lace and perfume—*(she laughs and looks at the perfume packages)*—I'm certain you give each other perfume for Christmas—He gives you Madame Rochas—And you give him Monsieur Rochas eau de cologne— deodorant—soap—aftershave and body lotion—so that he smells

76

and tastes the same everywhere.

Anne tries instinctively to hide the packages of perfume behind some of the other bags.

Beth: *(matter-of-factly)* But it still can't disguise the smell of garlic *(intimately)*—Do you fix snails, too, the way he tasted them in France? *(remembers with disgust)* First, you stand there and pick all those repulsive little animals out of the can and then you stick them into their own shells and cover them with garlic butter and put them in the oven—Just so that he can sit afterwards and pick them out of their shells again with a pair of tongs.
(She mimics his gestures when he is digging for a particularly well-hidden snail).

Anne starts laughing a little, nervous, girlish laugh which she can't stop.

Beth: *(laughs as well,disarmingly)* No—it's not nice of me to make fun—After all you love snails—*(thoughtfully)* I was the one who couldn't stand the smell of snails—boiled fish and garlic—It smells like—No—

(She interrupts herself and looks down thoughtfully, while Anne watches her expectantly. Then she looks directly up at Anne with warmth).—Actually I've missed you.

Anne gives her a surprised look.

Beth: Yes—Yes you visited us almost every day, you know—I realize I wasn't exactly pleasant to you all the time—But that was because

you always seemed so satisfied with everything—So disarming—
Sometimes I thought that you almost inhibited other people that
way—As soon as they approached, you became so polite and
friendly, at the same time, as though you were particularly frail and
delicate—It was as though you had found a kind of warm and
secure place—As though you experienced everything through a
down comforter.

*Anne starts at the words "down comforter". And bends down
deeply over the bags.*

Beth: *(continues a little hectically)* There wasn't any development in
your security—That's why I tried to provoke you sometimes—
Yes—It was for your own sake—It wasn't because I didn't like
you—*(thoughtfully)* That is to say there was one thing that really
did irritate me—I couldn't stand the way you always imitated me—
When I had blond, short hair you turned up with blond, short
hair—When I had saved up for a pink silk blouse you showed up
in a pink silk blouse the following week—Not a good color on you,
either—But you made it one—Since I drank Irish coffee you
developed a weakness for Irish coffee—Even in the summertime—
You borrowed all my books—And when you had read them we had
exactly the same opinions—Yes—Sometimes I was forced to
contradict myself—because I couldn't stand the way we always had
the same opinions—*(sarcastically)* But that didn't do any good—
You were quick to change your mind—Now I see that you did it
because you were unsure of yourself *(pause)* but then—I was afraid
of you—Sometimes I dreamed about you—You came and stroked
my face—You removed my colors—Your hands forced their way
under my clothes—and I was naked and white—I didn't have any
place to go.

78

Beth glances at Anne and attempts a little, ironic laugh.

Beth: Well—that's just about how it was—Isn't it?—*(pause)* I couldn't fight your accomodating nature—You played unsure—But really I was the one who was unsure—*(in wonder)* Why, you never showed any part of yourself.

Anne looks as though she is about to say something.

Beth: *(interrupts)* No—nonsense—That was just something I thought then—Why am I sitting here and saying it now—That isn't what I meant at all—Actually I learned a lot from you.

Anne looks at her, surprised and slightly flattered.

Beth: I got rid of a lot of bad habits—that little, charming laugh. *(She laughs a thin, coy laugh which resembles Anne's. She cuts it short and sweeps it away with a movement of her hand. Anne looks frightened and hurt. Beth continues sensibly.)* And I completely broke the habit of putting whipped cream in my coffee—Just think of all the calories you saved me from— *(pause in which she rationalizes thoroughly)* And when Bob and I got divorced—really it wasn't your fault at all—You certainly weren't the first—And besides Bob and I had agreed to be free—*(indulgently).* He needs to make an impression on a woman now and again so that he can feel his mane growing—No—the real reason we got a divorce was that I was getting the best and most demanding offers at that time—Yes—I even think I was earning the most money.

Anne is again very preoccupied with her list.

That was what he couldn't take—Yes—he tried to act happy, of course—And I always asked his advice about everything—But then I didn't always follow his advice—the way I had in the beginning— Yes—in a way it was a relief when you showed up—you sat there on the sofa with your big, soft, yielding eyes and thought that everything he said was intelligent—You helped him put the cups on the tray *(dryly)* since it was, after all, his share of the housework to make coffee in the afternoon—And if there was a button I didn't have time to sew on why there was nothing you liked better than sewing on buttons—Actually you freed us both from the guilty conscience we would have had, otherwise, about each other—When he was with you he didn't feel a bit demanding or chauvinistic or anything—nope—he was just oh so natural—But maybe you really only took over my old role—everything I was trying to free myself from—And what he saw in you was maybe not so much you as your ability to adapt—Sometimes I almost think I was the one who pushed the two of you into each other's arms—You think of course that I was inconsolable when he announced that now he was moving in with you—*(shakes her head)* That only lasted a couple of days—And you know what— Then I woke up *(eagerly and energetically)* First of all I had the walls torn down so that the whole apartment became one huge light room—I'd imagined it like that so often—And I discovered that there were loads of things I wanted to do and that I'd never thought about doing out of consideration for him—Bob doesn't like to travel for example—Suddenly I only had to do things for my own sake—I got up for my own sake and I went to bed for my own sake—And the meals didn't have to be ready on the dot anymore—just because he gets hungry on the hour.

Anne casts a nervous glance at her watch.

Beth: *(laughs)* And just to think—I stopped pulling in my stomach when I walked from the bathroom into the living room—And suddenly I didn't have to be afraid of using my experiences—The bad ones, too—in my work—When I went on stage I didn't have to be concerned about whether he would feel that I gave away too much about myself or was too immodest—I didn't have to be afraid of opening up old wounds—And I didn't have to take Bob's planned vacations into consideration—No—actually I'm not cut out to be married at all—I'd rather be in love—I like being warm and loving—but without any plans and definite agreements—And without giving up any part of myself—I don't want to hide the fact that I'm strong anymore—I don't sell my independence for security—Yes you think you're independent, too—You earn money—but your money is allowances and money for clothes and children's shoes—If there isn't enough to pay the mortgage it's his fault—But in return you go along on fishing trips "For the children's sake" you say—But also so that he won't find somebody else to go fishing with—You live according to his rules—He decides about the important things—Which friends the two of you are going to have—What purchases the two of you are going to make—What opinions the two of you are going to have—And you adapt within the big rules—you make your own little, tiny, completely intangible rules—a soft and swampy place where you dream that you're free—You never talk about it—You hide it— *(persuasively)*—Tell me about it—I'll understand.

Anne appears to be embarrassed and reluctant.

Beth: (appealing to Anne) My goodness—are you afraid of betraying yourself—Afraid of seeming just as frustrated as all the others— But *(with a glance at the shopping list and the pencil)* I understand that—Household accounts have a way of making even the most passionate love affair burn out—*(pause)*—But listen— don't you remember how open we were with one another then— How we could talk about everything—*(poised)* And that's why it was so easy, too—that Bob and I could part as friends— *(disappointedly)* But I admit I hadn't imagined that the friendship would come to an end at exactly the same time as the marriage— *(thoughtfully)*—Maybe it was because of you—No—you never oppose anything—At least not directly—*(pause)* But if I had had a child things would have been different.

Anne looks directly at her, surprised.

Beth: Yes—how I have envied all of you when you went around with big stomachs and looked like clumsy angels or cows—And everyone looked at you with tenderness—The way you always had someone to come home to—Someone to do things for—A dependence—a duty—and someone to talk to—But no—I don't regret it—It would have been selfish of me to have a child—I would have been an impatient and harassed mother—No—my body will never be a palace of fragile flesh—I don't want to be beset by hidden, mysterious life or by too many sleepless nights— I've made my choice *(without sentiment)* I get by on borrowing— after all there are enough children around—You can always borrow a child over the weekend while its parents are relaxing—But sometimes I look at their hands—their little, firm hands with dimples or folds—and I feel their firm, warm grasp—I wish that I could just keep on holding on to them and not have to let go all of a sudden—because they're borrowed—You know sometimes when I go out alone I feel as though I only see other people's hands—I see how they slip into each other, suddenly and trustingly—how nervous hands conceal themselves in other hands—And I see the little, impatient jerks on a sleeve—hands that want to go home—And nobody touches me like that—it's as if they were afraid of burning themselves on my skin—*(she looks down at her hands)* My hands—they're healthy—they're strong—normal and lonely—I can fold them in on themselves—clench them into fists or let them hang relaxed—Sometimes I stroke them myself—they're well-kept and soft—they don't do many dishes—I see other people walking hand in hand—No set dates—No surprises—completely calm—I go home alone—I let myself in all alone and stand for a minute with my eyes closed—it's as though all the walls were still there—then I walk quickly through the living room—*(pause)* No—I don't want for anything—All that stuff about being happy, it's just something you think you're missing—*(hesitating)* But maybe Bob was right, anyway, the time he said that a career can't replace a life—I don't know—I'm doing fine—But it doesn't matter to anybody—I don't take care of anything for anybody—I just take care of myself—I can travel wherever I want—nobody's waiting for me—And sometimes I can fly from winter to summer or from night to day—then I think it must be in the hours I gain or lose—A place in the sky—floating and unattainable.

It's as though she suddenly discovers Anne who has been watching her attentively the whole time.

Beth: *(laughs)* No—what should I be missing—But why don't you say something—Why are you just sitting there, letting me talk?—There isn't anything wrong, is there? *(spontaneously persuasive)*

Know what—Just this once, let's drop everything—Let's go over to my place—I'll do the shopping in a jiffy.

Anne looks hurriedly at her watch.

Beth: *(a bit dejected)* No—I understand, of course—You can't today because of the children—But we could make a date

Anne looks away, evasively, and flees into her purse, lists and bags.

Beth: *(gets up)* No—what would we talk about anyway *(she takes her time putting on her gloves and wrapping her scarf)*
But I might have been able to tell you something—Bob visited me once—It must have been right after Charlotte was born—you must have been very tired still—It was all over between you two—he said—It had been a mistake—He wanted to come back—I do believe he even used the word "home"—I stood and looked at him—his temples were higher—it looked touching, almost childlike—But I said no—For your sake—I said—And at that moment I felt noble—*(laughs)* but of course it wasn't on account of you—It was for my own sake—I knew I wouldn't be able to cope with it all again—Yes—if you had been able to—I would have admired you—envied you and wished that I were in your place—But now that I know that the two of you only stay together because you haven't got the courage to be alone—*(she disappears quickly)* Greet him from me and say that I'm doing fine—.

If It Really Were A Film

The most annoying part of it is that they look at him all the time that way. They talk about him, too. At times as though he were some kind of main character. And at times as though he weren't even present. They call him: defendant, boarder, swindler, violent criminal, husband, thief. They roll his days up and they spool them back and forth. As though it were a film they weren't quite satisfied with. And as though there were something or other they wanted to correct.

But that's not the only thing that makes him nervous. Their movements are there, too. The rustling of clothes, hands, purses, skin. A strangely dusty but nevertheless solemn gathering.

At times they also try to drag words out of him. And at times he really does talk, because otherwise the pauses would be much too long. But he doesn't like doing it.

If only the judge would stop looking straight at him, at the very least. If only the defense attorney and the prosecutor would stop addressing themselves so cooly and demandingly to him alone. If only he could just sit in a soft, dark auditorium with corduroy-covered chairs and a nice, smooth screen where everything happened.

If it really were a film. —How simple and easy it would be. Because really films are what he likes the most. The snug, protective darkness and the women who are so beautiful, so delicate and so moving. And they do everything. Much more than you can imagine. And they don't mind that he's watching. They're never offended. Not even when he talks to them.

Once he just whispered to Catherine Deneuve that he thought she had ugly legs. And she didn't produce one nasty remark in return. She just smiled—a little, nervous smile. Then she walked away between tall, sub-tropical plants. Arrogant, thin-legged and beautiful.

Actually he's never been unlucky in anything on film. Maybe the plot hasn't always suited him. But then he just closed his eyes and let it continue on another track. And on even the most unlucky days he's never had the slightest trouble with Sarah Miles or Charlotte Rampling. He's looked them straight in the eyes without blinking and without needing to excuse his appearance, his breath or the weak but unmistakable odor of sweat.

Otherwise there isn't much that turns out right. Not his marriage, either. But he still remembers what she looked like.

She packaged pastry shells. Her lambskin fur was greasy at the neck. She never shaved under her arms. They had a car and a two-room apartment with a toilet on the landing.

They took turns doing the shopping quickly on the way home. They ate at the kitchen table. She stuffed the food she felt like eating into her mouth with her fingers. Afterwards she sat there for a long time with her elbows propped up on either side of her plate. Luckily no children.

They read the sex-advice column together. Mostly she did. She read out loud. Slowly and clearly, as though it were homework. It didn't interest him very much. There weren't any pictures. He wrinkled his forehead while she read. There was something angular about her elbows and legs. And something Mediterranean about her hair and the bristling fur in her armpits. She wasn't, herself, particularly predisposed to sex. If they got around to it, then always in the same position. The missionary position. As far as he knew she wasn't very religious, either. Her knees pointed stubbornly up at the ceiling.

But she didn't love him any more, she said one evening, when she for once was sitting and knitting. The needles clicked up and down.

At heart he believed that she never had. Still he jumped up and ran out to the refrigerator. He took the aquavit bottle with him down to the car. As far as he could see she kept on knitting.

First he drank a little. Then he drove out to the harbor and stood there and stared. The water seemed so strangely lethargic and half-dead with oil spots and dirt.

Still it made him feel sentimental. Dirty or not. There was something about water. A cold, flowing darkness. And you could die from it. He saw himself in slow-motion. Jump—no, more like slip over the edge—and down—deep down. As in dreams. Regret's small, clear bubbles on the surface. A scream shut up in water. A secret shut up in his body. He hurried back to the car and drank most of the bottle.

Perhaps she was still sitting there knitting. Or picking her teeth with a needle. Thoughtfully—with no tears pouring down her cheeks. "Don't love anymore." No—tears weren't her style. Only with physical pain. The time she hit her knee. And the time she was stung on the thumb by a wasp. It was his fault, she said. He had tried to swat it.

They would never have been happy together. Not in the long run.

He drove. While everything stood quite still and sharp in his head the car drove with elegant, gliding rapidity up onto the sidewalk. Some frightened shadow cried out and pressed itself against the houses.

He found a parking place. He wanted to stop. But there was something there. There was a sudden crash and shudder. A darkness and a huge silence in his head. A soft fall through circular, rocking rooms. And something warm ran down his neck.

And out of the rocking rooms. Out of the soft, dizzy darkness came the picture of Helle. Something festively illuminated. Something shimmering pink, something that liked to laugh, something warm, and light-blue near-sighted eyes behind light-blue glasses.

He could still drive. The car and he, they were invincible.

He rang Helle's doorbell. He also rattled the mailbox a bit. She came out barefoot and heavy with sleep, wearing something transparent and pink that clung to her body. It looked as though she were walking around inside a red projector. Her hair was damp with sweat. She held her watch all the way up to her nose. "It's two-thirty," she said. And her pupils were surprisingly dark.

He tumbled in towards her. In an embrace or a fall they toppled over onto the carpet without bumping themselves very much. The pink lace scratched his face. He was dizzy and all the sex-advice columns ran through his head. She was full of openings and sleep and damp pink skin. She had thin, beautiful legs and a little ruptured vein, fragilely blue. He wanted to find her clitoris with his tongue. It ought to be pink—like hard candy. Some place or other. His glasses bumped into her knee. She had a soft, slightly sickly odor. She started fumbling with his zipper with sleepy, indecisive fingers. Her dog had woken up. It stood beside them and watched. It was a big mutt with wispy fur and a long, wolflike snout. "She must do this often," he thought. "Since it isn't biting or growling." Her sex was long-haired like the dog. They tumbled into a vase on the floor. The dog moved unwillingly. His trouser leg got wet. He pushed the fragments aside with his foot.

He turned towards her face. She gave a little scream. "Maybe she's having an orgasm," he thought, amazed and relieved at the same time.

"Are you a sight!" she said.

She was the one who was a sight. He must have hit her nose with his knee.

"Go and look at yourself in the mirror," she said. They went out together.

The blood was coming from him. From his chin. A thick, dark streak that ran slowly down his neck.

"You have to go to the emergency room," she exclaimed, hysterical and practical at the same time.

She poured some instant coffee into a cup. He couldn't drink it.

"What did you want from me, anyway?" she asked as he was on his way out the door.

He didn't drive to the emergency room. Compelled by totally absurd curiosity he drove back to the parking lot. And it was overwhelmingly big and full of white, confusing lines. The dizziness and the nausea rose up in him again. Everything caved in. And if it hadn't been for the owner and the policeman, both standing there with sharp, flapping cones of light, he would have crashed into the same car once again from the rear.

They looked after him.

The result was three weeks in jail. Three stitches. And a concussion. Moreover, he lost his driver's license. But that way he sort of put it all at a distance.

Starting over was harder. After the dizziness had decreased. After there was only a thin white scar. And after somebody else had taken over his job.

Just trying to find a room. The landladies' suspicion. "And not too much frying in the kitchen. And no socks in the bathtub. And not too many visitors." If he doesn't fall out with them right away it's certain to happen when they discover that he sits around at home all day. And that he eats without a knife and fork and keeps shoes, sheets and socks in the same drawer. In the space of two months he lives in a lemon-yellow, a purple and a grey room. He's thrown out of the grey room because the landlady finds a woman's hair in the butter dish. That's a lie. It's one of his own, quite personal hairs from the top of his head. But it's true enough that he pinched a pat of butter.

That day he stands again with his clothes in a blue shopping bag. There are snow flurries. The cold makes him furious and depressed at the same time. He happens to think of his former wife whom he may even still be married to. Her secure life barricaded behind yellow pastry shells and knitting needles. Maybe she still reads the sex-advice

89

columns. He pushes her away. He has to start fresh. He has to move on. That day, too, is a kind of beginning.

Luckily there's a bus coming. He's so close to the bus stop that he only needs to run a couple of yards. He gets into the warmth and buys a ticket. Soft and secure he drives through the shimmering whiteness, without any particular plan. And he enjoys it, until he suddenly feels dizzy and hollow and remembers that he hasn't eaten anything since that morning at six-thirty, when he buttered a dusty roll with a pat of borrowed butter.

He gets out at a summer house area. The snow is falling more thickly. There's already a thick layer that creaks under his shoes and hangs in clumps under the soles. He drags his feet forward. He turns his toes inward. He doesn't care. Nobody notices how he walks. He sneaks around a bit and looks at the expensive, closed houses. Through the shutters he sees only darkness. The locks are solid and he touches them without hope. Suddenly one of them gives way. "A guest house." he thinks. "An annex." He finds a light switch and is standing in a gigantic, ice-cold bathroom with a shower and mirrors and golden faucets. Astonished, he polishes his glasses on a thick towel. Outside he pushes a pine tree aside. But it jabs back and tips a load of snow onto him.

Later he finds what he might have been looking for. A lock with a fragile hinge fitting. He coaxes his knife under it and the lock falls into the snow. He opens. And it's a gift.

It's jangling-cold. But what hasn't he heard about houses. Cash. Cigarettes. Transistor radios. Thick, dark cigars. And maybe a secret trap door in the floor where you just stick your hand down among valuable bottles. He lifts up the rug. And pulls out drawers. Half a package of Kings and 27 kroner in a matchbox. "A middle-class house," he thinks and seats himself in the kitchen with a quilt over his legs and the oven turned on to 250 degrees. He reads old magazines without distinguishing between the novels and the recipes. And once in a while there's a beautiful woman in a thin bra. He becomes impatient and looks around once again and discovers the freezer.

Really he doesn't expect much of it. He's never bought anything other than sausage, Chinese egg rolls and frozen cod. But when he opens it there's an orgy of big, frozen lumps of meat which he tosses out onto the floor. There are also packages of spinach, beans, liver pate and strawberries in plastic bags. "Strange," he thinks. "They must be strange—The people who have all this stuff. A traffic accident, a divorce or just a trip. It must be impossible, somehow, with all this frozen meat." Then he breathes on his hands a couple of times and tosses a pork roast into the glowing oven. Everything else he dumps back into the box.

He walks around a bit with the quilt over his shoulders. In the mirror he sees himself as an Indian.

On the dresser there are some photographs. Probably the people who own the house. Nice people. Friendly, as far as he can tell. Children, grandchildren, lunches. Wet children's clothes and laughter. Bottles and glasses. Well-nourished hips and stomachs. They could have been his parents.

But his mother is still alive. His good-looking, single mother and her men-friends. Usually they slipped him a kroner and shut the door. But where could he go for one kroner. He waited outside. At last he got tired of always standing there. He moved back and forth between her and an aunt. Once when they were both tired at the same time he spent half a year in a home for children. She had a right to live, too, she said the few times she visited him.

The roast smells a bit strange. He checks it. The plastic has melted away. A dull-white, slightly bubbling film is spreading over the baking sheet. Of course he should have remembered to unwrap it properly. But aside from that it looks like a good, warm, browned roast. He finds

91

plates, knives, forks, glasses. There's something festive about it. If only he had something to drink. Pork roast and water. Pork roast and instant coffee. Pork roast and camomile tea. Pork roast and elderberry juice. That's what the house has to offer.

But he feels like drinking red wine, black currant rum and aquavit. It's Friday, he remembers. He has enough cash. And from the bus he noticed that kind of phosphorus-like light that can almost only mean a supermarket.

But if someone becomes suspicious. He looks at himself in the mirror. Supermarkets don't become suspicious and aside from the quilt there's nothing unusual about him. He checks the roast again. It looks almost done. He sets the table for two because the table seems to invite it.

Outside the cold hits him more sharply. More glass-like than he had expected. But he's made up his mind. His shoes leak. But he would walk throught ice and glass. And afterwards there'll be warmth and fatty meat and wine. He's blinded by the snow and thinks that he's gone in the wrong direction. But suddenly he's standing right in front of the market. The doors open when his shadow falls on them and he walks in, between the laundry powder, stockings and fruit.

Luckily he's not alone. He follows a young couple with a shopping cart. A delicate, blond woman wearing a long-haired fur. Maybe wolf. She reaches out towards all the shelves. She takes cans and meat, cosmetics, butter and diapers. Her lips are shiny red. She has pointed canine teeth and a gold filling. She keeps on lifting goods down from the shelves and putting them in the cart while the fur makes her gestures hairy and meaningful.

He walks right behind them. He keeps on expecting the man to discover the mountain in the shopping cart and say that's about enough. He watches her stock up on liquor, six bottles of white wine and a half-bottle of cognac. Then he's distracted by his own purchases. Portuguese with a screw-on cap and black currant rum on sale. He glides in beside a cash register where the girl has deep dimples. And it's over and done with.

The way back is easier. He has the wind at his back and can follow his own footsteps. "My footsteps," he thinks. "As though they were worth following." But he makes his way quickly. Soon he'll be sitting down with improbable amounts of steaming hot meat. He'll eat and drink until he drops. He'll let himself tumble into bed and sleep heavily, numbed by food and wine. And not caring whether he drops fat and hair on the drainboard.

There's the hedge. And the light in the narrow kitchen window is shining cozily and warming. He sees his own footsteps. But suddenly there are three sets. His own, turned towards him, and two strange sets. Two sets of new, fresh tracks that weave in and out of his. One pair of shoes is a little smaller than the other. He stops. In front of him he sees two figures wrapped up warmly in scarves and coats. The man in a soft hat and the woman in an imitation fur cap which is pulled down over her ears. At first he can't believe it's true. They turn to the right at the low pine hedge and head straight for the house without turning around. Just two heavy, lumpy shadows. Then he hears a little, sharp scream from the imitation fur cap. But that's the only uplifting thing he hears. Because he runs back to the bus stop with a bottle in each hand. And those two—of course they'll walk right in and plant their broad backsides on the kitchen chairs and devour the entire roast. Embittered, indignant and nervous. In any case the woman will probably be nervous and stare restlessly into the darkness while she cuts her meat into little pieces and drinks instant coffee or camomile tea. He only thinks the last thought when he has seen that he has to wait one-and-one-half hours for the next bus and there isn't even a bus shelter.

The Portuguese is bitter and ice-cold. Still he manages to empty it. He falls asleep in the bus and wakes up because he is talking in his sleep in a thick, rough voice. They throw him out at the last stop. And there's most of the night to go before the cafeteria opens and he can read the newspaper and start tramping around looking for a new room.

He takes the cheapest one from the woman who has intelligent toad-like eyes and loose, brown-spotted skin.

"Partially furnished," she says and points to a flat bed. "Don't you have any luggage?"

"It's in storage," he says.

"Three months in advance," she answers.

"One," he says and rustles two one-hundred kroner bills a bit.

She smooths them painstakingly before they vanish into the pocket of her apron.

He says he's a seasonal worker.

"Which seasons?" she asks.

But he closes the door and falls asleep immediately.

Three days later he gets a job delivering newspapers and he tip-toes out the door wearing a ski cap and an imitation leather jacket.

He's home again around eight.

"You look like some kind of thief—might scare a person," snickers his landlady.

In some of the apartment buildings he saves himself the trouble of going up and down the stairs by running through the connecting attics.

He runs through narrow, crooked passages where everything is dusty and dry. In one spot the pigeons fly freely in and out through the attic windows and breed, shit, coo and die. There's a fluttering and rustling of wings and beaks. And a stench of filth and eggs lost before their time.

In other places there were storage rooms. Rusty fragile locks separate him from boxes with cups and glasses, tattered books, copperware, heaps of coal, baby carriages, bowl and pitcher sets, treasures and rubbish, all crammed together.

"Recycling" it says on the front page of the newspapers.

"Recycling" pound his feet as he runs down the stairs.

He knows the attics inside and out. He knows where the light switches are. Where the exits are and where there are nooks you can hide in if anybody should appear. "The evening," he thinks. "The evening will be the safest."

He chooses a storage room where you can see a transistor radio through the crack. In the morning he takes note of everything. Sober and clear.

But in the evening it's all different. Already on the stairs his heart flutters like a bird. And even though he's wearing rubber boots there is a strangely living creaking in the wood around him.

He doesn't feel safe until he's standing in front of the storage room. His hands don't shake. The knife loosens the hinges quite easily. He pushes the door open and the flashlight pulls things out of the dark. The transistor radio, a gas mask, a meat safe, a pile of newspapers. The objects become very close and meaningful as he touches them one by one, very softly as if he could disclose their essence in that way. He has to sneeze. Three-four-five times with his hands pressed over his nose. He feels dizzy and is just about to run away. But he turns off the light and forces himself to remain standing in the dense, living darkness. And nobody comes running to investigate his intruding sneezes.

Quickly he tosses the transistor radio into a nylon bag. He also takes a candlestick holder which may be made of silver and a little blue plate.

When he's standing in the street he feels a kind of relief which he mistakes for a moment for a good conscience.

At home he tries out the radio. It works.

"Well—" says the landlady. "Things are getting homey—You've got music."

95

She invites him for a cup of coffee.

The candlestick holder and the blue plate fetch thirty kroner at the second-hand store.

Standing there with the money in his hand he has the feeling, for the first time in a long while, of being successful.

Later it gets to be a habit.

Two hauls a day. And never on weekends. In the morning he picks out an attic. In the evening around eleven, just when the midnight showings are about to begin, he tip-toes off. His landlady's sleep is indestructible. He hears her thick, heavy snoring. Toad snoring, hidden under a down comforter. She's hard of hearing and perfect in every way. He gives her a vase made of purple glass and a white porcelain dog that he couldn't get anything for, anyway. She grasps it with broad, gentle fingers. He hasn't even thought of wrapping it.

Little by little he learns what's worth taking.

One night he carries a box with old, fragile glasses wrapped in newspaper. He doesn't miss a single step.

"Where'd you get all this from?" says the owner of the second-hand store and looks at him curiously with reddish eyes in a fine, mouse-like face.

"—My mother—" he says. "She doesn't feel like keeping them any more."

The second-hand dealer unwraps the glasses carefully and holds them up to the light. He places them on the table as cautiously as if they still contained wine.

"If your mother has any more where these came from—"

He makes 300 kroner on the glasses.

Summer comes, hot and humid. Buzzing flies, dense grey dust and midnight showings. He can afford to sit in the sidewalk cafes and drink cool draught beer. He goes to the air-conditioned movie theaters. He wears light clothing. In the afternoon he carries a grass-green towel in his shopping bag. He undresses gently in the park and lies down and reads magazines. Once in a while he eats in a cafeteria or at a fast-food stand. He watches the girls. Their thin T-shirts and their long, smooth legs. He sniffs the scent of their body lotion and shampoo.

He expands his territory. In a suburb where he's never delivered as much as an advertisement he picks up fifty French canning jars. It's a sport. He carries them down two at a time. He has to take a taxi home. It's foolish and brazen. He makes 100 kroner and goes to Sweden in the afternoon. He gets drunk and grabs a girl with little Swedish breasts. He can't understand what she says. Otherwise everything is as it should be.

Sometime in the fall he gets carried away.

He sees an attic room stuffed with tools. A power saw. An electric drill. Heavy, hard things. He's seen in the newspaper what that kind of thing is worth.

For two weeks he doesn't take anything at all. He becomes restless and can't fall asleep. Everytime he closes his eyes he sees all those valuable tools in front of him, gleaming and dangerous like a hook that pulls him up into the light. And he gets up. He walks through the streets to tire himself out. He watches the couples who cling to one another. He sees a very tall girl who is almost transparently fair. Wearing tight blue jeans and a leopard jacket that's half-bald. She walks like a beast of prey; sinewy, thin and muscled. He passes close by her. Her jacket is open. Her blouse is glossy-black. Her belt is a dog collar. He tries to catch her eye. But she keeps on walking. As unapproachable as an advertisement.

He doesn't have the knife or the flashlight along. But he can't wait any longer. It has to be now, it must be now. He searches his pockets. The comb. Maybe that can be of use. Or he can just tip-toe up and look. Just look at it once more. That will make him feel more secure when it's for real.

He turns the corner. He moves toward his goal without taking notice of people or facades. There's a pounding in him like there was the first time. Then the darkness of the back stairs closes around him, soft and soothing. There are only his own, almost soundless, footsteps. And all the way at the top the small rustling sounds of the pigeons and the wind that rushes in through the cracks in the roof. He shoves the comb under the hinge. It gives way, willingly and tenderly. The door opens almost of its own accord. And the power saw and the electric drill are overwhelmingly heavy in his hands.

He doesn't turn on the light on his way down. Maybe that's the mistake. He's used to light and fragile glass. But the weight of the tools makes him unsure. It's as if it grows in the dark. A value that's far too big and far too cold and smooth. He leans against the wall for a moment. He starts to count the steps. That's what seems wrong. If only he had never counted. If he hadn't expected six and been surprised by the seventh. He stumbles in the dark. He twists his ankle but gets up again and continues. Then suddenly there is light on him. Blinding and white. It cuts into his eyes. All the way into his head.

"What the hell!" says a gigantic man.

And the power saw drops from him and down the stairs with a deafening crash.

The man presses him against the wall and doesn't say anything other than "What the hell!" while he stares at him as if he were some sort of strange insect that annoys him because he can't just go ahead and kill it.

The rest is just routine. A relief almost when the giant's wife gets hold of the police. In the car he takes a breath.

He's tried this before. But then he was almost numb. This time everything is completely clear. The steel comb. The light. The saw that fell down the stairs, the electric drill that he, idiotically enough, held onto tightly. Kept holding onto. No matter how hard the giant squeezed.

He is torn out of his darkness. Up into the cold, smooth light. He sees a man at a desk. The man looks healthy and suntanned. He probably has a wife, children, apartment. Maybe a house—car—pension.

The man looks at him. In a much more friendly way than he feels he deserves. And it's so easy to confess to the power saw and the electric drill.

The machine clatters it down.

"But there must have been more—What was your specialty?" It sounds almost polite and interested.

"French canning jars—"

"Residence?"

If he had such a perfect nose. Such fair, smooth and shiny hair. Such eyes that inspired confidence, without any structural defects. And that height.

"And you were moving about in the area between eleven and eleven-thirty?"

He had no reason to deny it. The man smiles as though they were friends, in a way. Or as if they could become friends at the very least.

"Do you know Miss Marion Levinsen?"

And it's easy. It's just like that time with the car. The same sparkling dizziness and relaxation. Of course that's her name. She approaches like an elegant, tame beast of prey. With her elegant nose in the air. With her tight, tight pants. Her platform heels that make her walk artificially challenging and difficult. The weight even though she isn't heavy. She's transparent and hard like a piece of glass. Cool, infant and delicate. The long, thin neck raised high above the worn, leopard-skin collar. The fair, bleached hair with an artificial phosphorus-like tinge. Rough. Delicate. Beautiful. With dark, half-open lips.

"You're the one who killed her. The theft of the electric drill and the power saw was supposed to be an alibi. We'll forget about the marmalade jars."

That's the way it must have been. Once again he sees her in front of him, the dog collar around the thin, fragile waist. Without sweat. Without sticky pink nuances. Without movement. With her arms stretched over her head. With smooth armpits. Fleeting dark shadows under her eyes. Long, glossy, almost red-brown nails. And otherwise white. White, shiny bones under white, fragile skin. The distinct outline of her hip bone. The dark hollows over her collarbone. Blows to her hips. Teeth in her breasts, in her white, bitter skin. Her moth-wing lips. Quivering for a moment in the light. And she's gone.

"Have there been any others?"

It's a strange confidence he seems to deserve.

Helle emerges from her pink light. The Swedish girl's breasts. His wife's monotonous, schoolgirl voice, women who scream on film and suddenly, with one single simple and well-directed movement, lie completely still.

The man looks at him the whole time, interested and without reproaching him. And he talks and talks, until his brain is emptied of pictures and they take him away.

The cell isn't noticeably worse than his last room. But he feels worse. The regularity of the meals is an imposition. He skips some of them and loses weight. Outside they're all lucky. Outside there are still buses in the streets. Outside there's the old, corroded sound of transistor radios. And you can pop into a movie theater whenever you please and find the glow of successful luxury. Or you can buy a beer at a sidewalk cafe and for just a short time feel above all the others who walk by. He longs to get out. He longs to get on.

He hopes that he'll be called to the big desk.

One day a defense attorney appears.

"I don't believe you—" says the defense attorney and gives him a mildly reproachful look. "—I think you're trying to put one over on us—"

He's about to say that he doesn't care for that tone of voice. But on the other hand he doesn't want the man to leave, either.

The defense attorney's sweater has a little run at the edge. He thinks that if he takes hold of the little thread, very cautiously, and pulls while the attorney is staring straight ahead with his mild, preoccupied eyes, he might be able to unravel the whole sweater.

"You've confessed to nine incidents of violence.—I've talked to your wife. To your landlady and to one of your female acquaintances. They say that it can't possibly be you."

"What do they say?"

"Your landlady says you're a nice, sociable person."

"She doesn't know the first thing about it."

"Your wife says you're incapable of cooking up anything at all. Your former girl friend says you have a problem you can't quite formulate. Regarding Miss Levinsen—nobody saw you in her vicinity. And none of her acquaintances have ever met you."

He's dizzy.

"Withdraw your confession," says the little nondescript man. "You confessed under duress or out of confusion. You weren't accountable for you actions."

"At the moment of the crime—" he says, relieved.

"No," says the lawyer, almost irritated. "You haven't done anything. You're just a perfectly common thief."

One day Helle shows up.

She looks at him with round, gentle eyes behind the fish scales of her new contact lenses. She's put on weight. Her breasts are heavy behind something flimsy and pale and purple.

"The newspapers are writing a lot of shit about you," she says.

101

"—What do they say?—"

"Loads—But I don't believe any of it—I just think there was something that you wanted to say."

"And what might that be?"

"I want to help you," she says.

He looks at her breasts, much too round and much too big.

"Don't you think you put too much flour in the gravy?" he says.

Later they come and get him.

They ask him questions while he sits all the way up front in the auditorium with the small rustling sounds of the audience behind him. His head aches the way it usually does when he sits too close to the front.

He hears the dry, boring voice of his attorney saying that he's nothing but a common thief.

They also call him: defendant, boarder, swindler, violent criminal, husband, thief.

They contradict one another.

They roll his life up and they spool it back and forth. His wife, his landlady and Helle are in it. And he wishes they would turn out the lights so that it would just be dark and soft.

One day the defense attorney gives him a picture of a blond woman with dark lips and a smile that's both guarded and hard.

"Who does this represent?"

It feels strangely flat in his hand. He doesn't know what to answer.

But he can sense that they wish he would say something. So that the film can continue.

He has the feeling that everything around him is tense. He's like an arrow on a bow. In a moment he'll say something. He'll give way under the pressure and fly towards unknown landscapes. Passive and hard.

He has to say something.

102

The Wax Doll

My hands are as frail as a child's. My nails are long and narrow. My hand rests on the pillow. Clenched, as though it contained a secret. I open it. It's empty.

This is the first morning in which I see my husband's face. Sleep has made it more mysterious, but also helpless and soft. The fleshy nose. The bushy eyebrows. It certainly isn't a beautiful face. Well yes.— The eyes might seem beautiful and calculating. His body.—It's a well-kept, polished body. Like his shoes.

Our perfume stands in tall cut-glass bottles on the dressing table. Our clothes lie on the sofa. We undressed slowly. We were both signed, from the outside to the inside, by the most famous fashion designers. We laid aside our works of art. Each and every detail was exquisitely beautiful. We were almost numb from the trip and the wine. But still we took great pains. We laid everything in the proper folds. And all the while we didn't speak.

The thin curtains flutter a bit. Sweep over the floor. A fly buzzes, simmers, caught in a fold. And that's the only trace of disorder or life.

Outside lies the city. The streets stretch themselves out, ready to receive us with their statues, their fountains, trees and spiced scents. We'll make love with blisters on our feet and sleep and dream perfect dreams in wide-screen. It'll be easy. Even on charter trips sudden friendships, infatuations, fatherings and motherings are far more common than poisonings. Anything can happen when you travel.

My hands are small and frail. They can't hurt a fly. They're free. My hair falls free.

My long smooth arms. My stomach. My legs are free.

Or maybe not?

My husband's hands are the hands of a rich man. They're firm. The nails are polished. And the fingers are a little crooked, as though they always have to clutch their property or their quarry. He doesn't take off his rings when he sleeps.

I've known other hands. Smooth perfect hands. Without sweat. Without the slightest nervous tremble. I left them behind. I've surrendered myself to these short hairy hands with nails that are polished by a strange woman. They ought to smell of gold. Crocodile skin and gold.

That's the kind of thing that makes me soft.

No.—It wasn't the designer clothes or the ring or the fur.

It was because he decided.

He decided where we should meet. What we should eat and drink and when I should lay aside my cigarette. It was so easy.

In the beginning I planned that I would rebel. That next time I would say something haughty and ice-cold while I, with admirable ice-cold gestures, destroyed my cigarettes in his onyx ash tray.

But I didn't do it. I relaxed.

Maybe I could have developed. Maybe I could have acquired a longing spirit and extravagant melancholy eyes.

But I just wanted to be happy. Quite ordinary and without too much bother.

It smells very faintly of lemon in here, as though someone has walked through the room without leaving any other evidence behind. No. The smell must come from outside. Or from one of the cut-glass bottles. Or from the soap. Or the towels.

If I could sleep.—Run away.

If I could fall asleep and never wake up. Or if I could wake up to something else. If I could wake up and be myself as a baby. If I could,

104

once again, stretch out my hands and get everything.

I was an obese, arrogant baby.

I merely had to press my broad face to the crib bars and they picked me up. I merely had to open my mouth and they filled it with milk, soft ice cream, caviar, lemon drops. They filled my bed with stuffed animals. They filled the room with multicolored pictures and the closets with fur-lined coats and shoes.

I was a secure and protected baby. They gave me everything. They guessed my wishes before I had managed to figure out for certain what I wanted. Sometimes I felt disappointed—or maybe tired would be better—when I opened the packages containing big fragile dolls that I had merely cast a fleeting glance at in a display window.

They loved me unreservedly. They were boundless.

I remember once. It was on a big open square. My mother had misunderstood my wish for ice cream. She handed the wrong kind. And it made me furious and I hit her in the face. But instead of pulling her face away she bent down closer and closer to me. While ignoring the blows she asked, undisturbedly loving and solicitous, what kind of ice cream I wanted. And I kept on hitting and hitting and couldn't stand it. And the pigeons flew away. And people stared at us. And it was impossible to say the name of the right kind of ice cream. That's what my parents' love was like.

I couldn't comprehend how they had made me. Especially after I realized what the motions of copulation were. They worked together during the day. At night they went to separate rooms. There was an intercom between them. "The intercom—" I thought. "It must have happened over the intercom." It was impossible to imagine that the inside of my parent's bodies could be passionate cryptic landscapes of blue, green and red like the posters at school. Or that they ever could have spoken a sighing, moaning language. I imagined that they were made entirely of paper.

But they loved me. They wrote my essays and they did my math when I couldn't do it myself. They invited children for me to play with. They sneaked along on my first date so that they could comfort me immediately if I was disappointed. And when I was eighteen they gave me a car with white fur upholstery. It was like snuggling up to a fat white bear that growled when I drove.

Little by little I became more independent.

There was a lot to learn.

I had to learn to move gracefully—also outside of the car.

To eat more or less properly—without belching.

I learned that it's possible, just by lighting the right brand of cigarette with a very fast or a very slow, almost gentle gesture, to express arrogance, sensitivity or sorrow. Much more easily and with far fewer obligations than if one used words. I also learned to do arithmetic. To dance. And that it's possible, with just one little glance, to get the waiter to bring a bowl of ice cubes.

I learned that by being insolent one can sometimes give the impression of being both tempermental and liberated.

I also learned to speak foreign languages. To get into and out of airplanes. But first and foremost I learned to be exclusive.

It took time.

"Take care of your sun-tan."

"Take care of your hair."

"Protect the polish on your nails. Accentuate their perfect half-moons."

"Let the rouge give your face a glow."

It took great effort. And the fever in the dressing rooms when I was searching for the right blouse, the right fur cap, the right boots. When I tried them on again and again so that I wouldn't make a mistake and be forced to give the lace, the silk and the leather away to charity.

106

Yes, my sensitivity. My nervousnes. My fear was in those purchases.

My joy and sensuality was in the soft fabrics when they were draped around my body.

My personality was in the colors that belong to me. The dusty colors—the mixed colors—rose-pink, lavender, mauve, olive, purple, almond and black.

But never clear red. Clear blue. Or white.

And ticklishness, my excitement was in the hairdresser's little sharp scissors when he made me vital, new and interesting.

But I was still the child of my parents. The child of my father the accountant and my mother the secretary.

I lived with them. I ate with them. Sometimes I answered the telephone for them and sealed their envelopes. My days were like pearls on a string: smooth, perfect and a bit boring.

But it all seemed temporary. As if I were just waiting for the chain of perfect days to break. For something, or rather someone, who would come and make everything exciting and intense. Even standing in front of the mirror stroking my face with rouge and glittering shadows to highlight the best of cheekbones, nose and too childish mouth, even that seemed like a kind of waiting.

"Just take your time," my mother said.

"Just figure out what really interests you," my father said.

"Tell us what you really want."

But I didn't know what that was. I only knew my good points and my bad points. My curves and my colors.

We traveled together. My parents and I.

We traveled to big, simmering cities together. I can remember their names. Otherwise I've forgotten them.

We lay on the large, white beaches. The colored leaves didn't cast shadows on my face.

We ate in restaurants with a view of the sea.

I noticed how people looked at us when we walked into a hotel reception area. It was like a prickling in my neck. And I felt both arrogant and shy.

But there's only one event I really remember.

One night I was staying in a room that faced the street. I thought I heard noise. A woman's voice, slight and eager. And a little later a man's voice. I went over to the window and looked down. The woman was young and thin. She was wearing a short, pink skirt that sort of quivered around her long, thin legs. A black shawl dripped down over her shoulders and her throat was very white.

The man was walking very close beside her. She talked and talked. Suddenly he hit her across the mouth. And her voice flew towards the windowpane like a bird. She walked on with stooped shoulders.

I kept on remembering her, even though she wasn't either well-dressed or beautiful.

Otherwise I generally only remember women who are more perfect than I am. Women with greasy hair and poorly sewn trousers annoy me—they're wasting their beauty resources.

But I kept on remembering that young woman. Behind my closed eyelids she kept on walking through the dark, down at the bottom of the city. And her voice was in all of the high, unexpected sounds that frightened me. In some way or another she must have had style. Because that's what I see in a woman.

With men it's different. I don't know their style.

I like their admiration. It makes me feel sure of myself. Like a mirror.

But their long, sloppy confidences, their adhering eyes and fumbling caresses all glance off my skin. They don't make me uneasy.

There was only one man who made me uneasy.

It was at a party. I don't remember any more what was being

108

celebrated. I didn't know much about the people who were giving the party. It was very late and I stood at the bar drinking from a tall, thin glass. The floor was a mess of cigarette butts, half-wilted flowers and sleeping people.

I drank my wine in little, tiny mouthfuls and decided to go home as soon as I had finished my glass.

A man approached me. He looked confident and important even though he was shorter than me. And his breath was by no means pleasant.

He took me by the arm. Together we walked into the garden. There was thick, soft snow everywhere.

I felt his hands on my temples. My face and my shoulders. I felt the blood behind my skin. I knelt in the snow. I drank his semen. Like a baby with thin, gulping sounds. I didn't see him again.

Other men had been mirrors that glided past. I had avoided their hands and their smell. I only remembered this man. His smell. His sex, his hands. I remembered it so clearly, as if it were something I had dreamt. And in the mirror I searched for a mark on my face. A wrinkle. A trembling. A wound.

"Take care of yourself and your appearance."

"Be arrogant. Be calm. Be beautiful."

"Fill in the curved line with smoke-blue."

"Buy lace. Buy silk. Buy rouge. And remove the hairs that disfigure your beauty."

Spring came bringing far too much light. Summer came bringing hot, restless nights. I could feel that my body was heavy and stiff and somehow without feeling, except for the dry pricking on my back where the sun had burned. I couldn't sleep. I went to bed half-numbed by wine or pills. But every time I was about to drop off into sleep something immediately happened. A sound or just the smell of my own perfumed sweat made me wide-awake again. And I found myself in a cramp-like waking state, like a fish flopping in the light, while I longed simply to sink down into the soft depths of sleep.

I got up. I drank milk. I smoked. Sometimes I thought about finding a knife or a razor blade and opening a vein or two. Then it would all disappear. My irritation. My perfectionism. My footsteps. My thin yawning while reading Vogue and Harper's Bazaar. The long cigarettes with the red print of my lips. And the feeling that all that wasn't enough, anyway.

But of course I didn't do it. Not seriously. I tried to cut myself in the ankle a bit. My blood was much lighter in color than I had imagined. That frightened me. Maybe I was, in reality, afraid of sleep, too, afraid of silence and phosphorus-shining dreams.

I never really figured it out. There's so much I've never really figured out. But it was the day after such a night that I met Jan. It was a day on which I hated the circles under my eyes and could only think about finding a cool, lonely place.

"Wax Museum" I read on a sign. There was something quiet and cool in those words. I went in.

I looked at all their gods and queens. There wasn't anything that impressed me. I walked fast. But when I reached him I stopped. He pointed the way. But I remained standing just as still as him.

I didn't merely gaze at the dry, perfect hand that didn't tremble at all. I saw his whole person. His essence.

Famous movie stars had been the models for his face. His shoulders are the whole of Greek culture. His ankles. Yes, even his knees are beautiful. His skin is cool. You can stroke it and stroke it. No smells stick to the tips of his fingers. Well yes—maybe a very faint odor of lemon.

I didn't think of him as a doll. And it was only when I was sitting with my foot on the accelerator that I remembered all those old stories about people who have been turned into dolls. And dolls that come to life. But stories are inescapable, I drove back.

He looked at me without dropping his eyes. His eyes are green with a tinge of ocean and emeralds.

I mirrored myself in him.

The floor mirrored us. We looked good together.

He smiled. His smile is gentle and sharp, as though he sees through me. And I didn't have to react against it. I didn't have to find gestures, words, explanations to justify myself.

His chest is raised and lowered by deep, calm breaths that don't pass over his lips. I laid my head against that chest. I wanted him. It was easy. It was only a matter of money.

That very day I offered the owner of the museum a suitable sum. I picked him up in the evening. He stood up in the truck. His forehead brushed the plane trees in front of the carport. I was happy.

Of course I've had lots of dolls. Baby dolls with high-pitched nerve-wracking crying. Dolls that could walk, drink, sleep and wet themselves. And I've poked them in the eyes, lost them, dressed and undressed them and put them to bed.

But none of them have radiated arrogance and calm. None of them have been anything other than glass and paper-mache.

He was the first one I could love. And I owned him. I gave him a name and sexy underwear and cashmere sweaters and shoes. I could throw my arms around him and control my own rape while I listened to my own voice rising and rising in cascades of glittering, splintering sounds. Rising like a bird towards a windowpane.

Occasionally we got tangled up together. And I thought I was going to die. But that must have been on purpose as well because he was easier to steer than a car. But I let everything happen because nobody knew anything about it and because I saw in his green, conscious eyes that he desired it, too.

No.—He's a doll. His skin is chemical and dry. My hands and my

111

skin made it feel alive. My perfumes gave it fragrance. And my sweat that fell shining on his shoulders.

And yet.—I hadn't known before that there were so many dreams in my skin. I only knew its flaws and its smoothness.

What am I?

Is my soul in the smoke that slips out of the thin, white cigarettes?

Or is it in the sweat that runs down my temples in the softly-lit dressing rooms?

Or is it to be found in the high-pitched, bird-like cries? Or in the perfume that rises hot and spiced from my skin?

No. If there were something like that between him and me we would have a common soul. A smooth, passionate, beautiful, exhibitionistic and very shy soul that we shared.

Why should his skin be inferior because it's made of wax? His skin is more flawless than mine.

Why should his glance be unimportant because it's of glass? With him I could be myself in each and every gesture instead of just expressing the most graceful, the most pleasant and attractive parts of myself.

I never had to be ashamed of the words I mumbled into his perfect ears. He would never laugh at me. Talk about me to others. Or turn my words against me in an argument.

And yet I left him.

I didn't do it against my will. Nobody has ever demanded that I do something against my will. But in spite of that I wasn't the one who decided.

It happened by accident. It was certainly by accident that my father had invited a man who wasn't quite so young to dinner. He sat at our table and didn't take his eyes off me. He watched me attentively as though there were something about me he didn't understand or maybe even that he was critical of.

Maybe I was holding my fork the wrong way. But if I hold something the wrong way at least I do it with style.

He watched me over the meat and over the round, soft peaches we fished up out of the sweet wine. He watched me over the mocha. I drank my cognac too quickly and couldn't shake his eyes off me. We didn't say anything to one another. We only exchanged commonplace, polite remarks. He and my father did the talking. They talked about economics, future economics, I believe. I didn't know anything about it. I thought about reading the books in my father's office. But I didn't get around to it and I knew just as little about future economics the next time I met him.

My father had invited him again. By chance I was at home. If you can call it by chance that I was always at home. He still watched me over the roast beef and over the fruit that shone that evening in transparent jelly. That evening he asked me out. I said yes. Maybe because I couldn't, at that moment, think of any reason to say no.

Jan's eyes mirrored me as they usually did. But he wasn't any help to me. Neither of us knew how I should be dressed for this occasion. I didn't want to display my most provocative beauty. Just that part of it that might be attractive to a man who had thin lips, bushy eyebrows and wasn't so young anymore. I wanted to be delicate, graceful and elegant. I tried the little after-five dresses with the appropriate jewelry. But they were too ladylike. I tried the long, tight leopard-skin pants. And the long skirts. But all of them were wrong. When the taxi arrived I was wearing black and gold. I put a soft fur jacket over my shoulders. When I walked past the mirror I was older than I usually am.

It was different going out with him than going out with my parents. He didn't ask what I wanted to eat or to drink. He ordered wine and venison and spicy salads. Dishes I normally wouldn't have eaten. I want to know exactly what's in the food and just the thought of finding buckshot in a piece of meat can make me sick.

113

He told me about his marriage and particularly about his divorce. He talked about a richly furnished house, a summerhouse and two cars and a marble bathroom. She had suddenly left all of it.

"Can you see why?" he asked.

I wasn't used to drinking such heavy wines. I shook my head slowly, it hurt, and I felt depressed and soft.

In the taxi on the way home I started whimpering and sobbing out loud as though it were caused by an allergy.

"It's marble or plastic," I said to the driver. "I'm allergic to marble or plastic." But he didn't care.

I fumbled my way up the stairs. My boots made every step an obstacle. As soon as I got inside I lay down on the floor. The room spun around and I didn't know where it ended. But I fell asleep instantaneously. Without removing my make-up. And without taking off my fur jacket or my boots. No, I wasn't used to such heavy wines. I slept a cramp-like sleep with my little purse clutched tight under my arm.

In the morning I was the only one who sensed that Jan had turned against me. He observed me with innocent astonishment.

When I got up I was still a bit dizzy. And I promised myself that I would never do it again. Be together with someone else, only to feel alone. "No," I said as I brushed my hair. "No," I said as I pulled off the gold-wrought boots. "No," as I cleansed my face. "No, he's certainly no hero."

A week later he asked me out again. I said yes. But I planned to enjoy myself this time.

But he didn't dance, he said. And after dinner I sat and gazed out over the round, shining, silver-colored dance floor where the couples moved past close to us. Wrapped around one another or maintaining a suitable, casual distance between one another. Their faces were blank.

"They are really stupid," I thought. I toyed with my drink. I was

114

terribly warm in my fur jacket. And I thought about all the beautiful, dead animals that had been sewn together just to cast a soft, flattering light on my face.

That evening he went up with me.

We took off our clothes with slow movements, as though it were an agreement we were forced to keep. I closed my eyes. I put my nails in his back. But I didn't feel him.

He left before my parents woke up. Fleetingly and indifferently he pointed at Jan as though he were a chair or a bouquet of flowers.

"What's that thing for?"

"He's beautiful," I said. "He's got style."

"Wax mannequins aren't beautiful," he said indifferently. "They're vulgar."

But he was lying, because he didn't understand a thing. He was uninterested in beauty. He was incapable of stopping when he saw it. Not unless it was signed.

And me.—I had responded as coolly indifferently as if it really were only a wax figure. As if I didn't know that we were a triangle. Jan, the man and I.

It was the man and I who moved with pointed, mechanical movements. In and out of cars. Up and down stairs. Back and forth through doors. We were active and provocative with our laughter, our drinks, the cigarettes we smoked quickly, and above all with our words. It was Jan's nature to be calm, confident and gentle. He had no voice. No tears. But he had a being.

I couldn't grasp the man's nature. Sometimes I thought there was nothing more to him than criticism, reserve and deliberations. As though he were always doubting whether or not he liked me.

My voice, my breasts, my hair, my clothing. It was a though everything has to be appraised, and by standards that I didn't know.

My language, for example. My bad pronunciation of foreign words.

My soft, loving cooing: "Beloved," "Sweetheart." They were necessary for me, those kinds of words. A kind of insurance. But he felt they were insufficient. Just like my knowledge of music and art.

Once we went into a museum. It was solemn and dusty and very quiet. There were large figures that had clumsy legs and their skin seemed somehow grainy. The women's breasts were far too heavy, their ankles too thick, and even their hair was of stone.

"They're unnatural," I said.

"They're expressive," he said.

They frightened me. None of them expressed friendliness. I couldn't find one single obliging statue. They were all engrossed in something or other. In mutual love. In a fight. A hunt. Seen in relation to them I was superfluous.

But I couldn't explain it to him. No more than I could explain to him the gentleness of a piece of silk.

I always took great pains. Maybe it was his respect, in reality, that I wanted. To be mirrored admiringly just once by those overly particular eyes. And then keep on going.

There were still nights when I pressed myself against the smooth wax skin. Nights when I dreamed.

When I woke up I could tell that Jan had moved. He had turned his head towards me. He had lifted his arm a bit. His breathing was like a kind of sighing.

To turn one's head. To lift one's arm. To breathe. Were those movements that he always made? Or was it due to a passing car or my over-excitement? I stroked and stroked his skin. He smelled very clean while he decayed. It wasn't age or wear that made the blond hair fall out. The decay was a sign of life. He was mourning because he couldn't do anything. He had no characteristics other than his gentleness and his beauty. Everything else was something I had to start.

I played. I balanced between the two. I knew all along that it had to

116

end some day. But I couldn't pull out of it. I couldn't do anything other than wait.

One day the man asked me to marry him. And a ring with tiny, sparkling stones slid over my finger.

Still, I didn't say yes because of the ring. It was because it all seemed like a smooth and brilliant pattern that I fitted into.

We ordered the trip. The clothes. The food. The date. It was so easy.

Even my parents took it well. I had thought that they would cry. But they smiled. They poured wine. They waved. As though they fitted the pattern, too. As though they had been waiting for precisely this to happen.

I doubted whether they really cared for me. Maybe they had only wanted a little, well-nourished child. They could part with the grown-up child as easily as if I had been a used thing. Maybe they were already thinking of the brand-new babies that would grow inside my body.

"You're the right age," they said.

I looked at my hands. Inside there are lines and furrows that cross each other. Inside the hand is a complex landscape. But it is little and soft like a child's hand. And I'm no older than my hand.

My hands didn't tremble as I dressed. I had locked the door. I didn't want anybody to help me. I was cultivated, delicate and elegant.

Jan stood in the bay window. The sun slanted into the room. He smelled of cool perfume—the whole room smelled of lemon—but his skin was burning warm. His breathing was subdued and irregular, as though something was shattered. I didn't see his face.

Perhaps I was afraid that he would look at me in a coolly appraising manner. Or suddenly show anger or defiance. No, it wasn't that. I slammed the door shut behind me. I was running away. But I wasn't running away from him.

I missed him when I walked up the aisle in the smooth, white dress. When I got into the airplane and fastened the seat belt. When I bored my nails into the flowers to see if they were artificial. And when the photographers tossed the flashing of their cameras at us. I missed him.

When I see my husband's face I think of myself. And I stand very close to the mirror to see what effect he has on me. Perhaps a softness, a wrinkle, a flaw. It's not visible yet.

When he speaks I admire his words. I don't always understand his opinions. But they're impressive. Like putting your foot in a shoe that's much too big and heavy. And not knowing whether there's something pointed and sharp in it.

I'm scared. I feel like boring my nails into all of the white and red flowers. I feel like opening all of the cut-glass bottles.

His hands touched my shoulders. I felt the sharpness of my shoulders. The bones inside them. And I was afraid of dying. I was afraid of laughing until I became hysterical. I longed for a scream that would have to come from far away. From the colored landscape of dreams.

We fell asleep, numbed by the trip and the wine.

It was the fly that awakened me.

Or the strong odor of lemon that a third person could have brought along into the room without leaving any other evidence behind. The balcony faces out onto the street. Onto the city where we are going to walk soon, between the statues, fountains and flowering trees. In the city where everything is possible. The room shows no trace of disorder or life.

My hand is closed as though it holds a secret. I open it. It's empty. There are only all those thin lines that confuse me when I look at them.

There isn't as much as a twitch in my husband's face.

There's no breath from his mouth.

I touch his skin cautiously. It's cold and smooth.

118

I stroke his back. But my hands can't make him warm. Under his shoulder blade there's a very narrow wound. My hand is sticky with blood. The scream comes from far away. Closer and closer. Maybe it's flying out of my mouth.

A Day Off In The Clouds

The all-clear sounds and Mitzi leaves her parents' house. She sniffs the air through the white face mask. In her hand she carries a soldier doll with a spacesuit, parachute and flame-thrower and a little old-fashioned pair of binoculars. She swings it back and forth. Her movements are carefree and today is a surprise. There's neither fallout nor clouds. The earth is clean and grey. And the sky continues straight up. Today you could fly or go riding. For an instant she thinks about horses with light coats and long soulful faces. She jumps up and down. She kisses her doll. The red heart-shaped first aid kit bounces against her breasts. She caresses her cheeks and her throat. And her arms where she's made blue hickies. She turns to the right. She counts seven steps and five stones. At stone number five Kitty appears carrying her blond mannequin doll in her hand. They kiss each other through the thin fabric of their face masks.

"It's wide open today," says Kitty and looks up. "A day off in the clouds—"

Very cautiously they remove the masks and gaze at one another's faces.

Kitty has sunken cheeks and a little sweet mouth.

Mitzi's skin is cream-colored and soft.

Kitty drops her eyes and gazes painstakingly at the ground.

With lazy soft movements Mitzi drops down on her stomach in the dust. She puts the binoculars up to the soldier doll's eyes. She disguises her voice: "Zone number three is momentarily in serious danger—No reason to panic—Everyone will be evacuated—Zone

121

number four—Everyone should seek shelter temporarily in fall-out shelters and basements—"

"Come on," she says gently and pinches Kitty on the calf.

"I don't dare—I'm not allowed to—" says Kitty. "If I get anything on me—"

"It doesn't smell—It isn't dusty—It's *not*." says Mitzi and pinches harder.

"—But—my Mom'll go crazy."

"She is already," says Mitzi and enjoys the color that shoots up into Kitty's unprotected cheeks. "Nothing will happen—You get used to it—like the flies—That's what my Dad says—"

"Your kids will have six legs," says Kitty and her voice is suddenly glossy and arrogant.

"I'm not gonna have kids—I'm just gonna have a good time—" Mitzi smiles phlegmatically.

"At the very least you'll get a bad complexion and be depressed." stammers Kitty.

"Nothing else—" sighs Mitzi and looks coldly at the tears that pour down Kitty's nose.

"And pins in your stomach—" The voice flutters like a sparrow.

Mitzi knocks Kitty down by pulling just a little on her legs. Kitty falls backwards. Her voice flies up high. The tears run down her cheeks and a clear bead hangs on her nose.

"Kitty-cat" whispers Mitzi and presses her down towards the ground. "Fraidy-cat—little kitten—"

Kitty's hair is full of dust.

Mitzi puts her head on Kitty's chest and listens to the heart that flutters there. She imagines that it's a little red bird and that the ribs are curved bars. She puts her hand over Kitty's mouth so that she won't be disturbed.

Kitty bites with little sharp teeth.

Mitzi sticks an elbow in her chest and squeezes Kitty's nose as hard as she can. "Brat-cat—Are you finished now?"

"Ouch—Ouch—Yes—" Kitty's legs whirl up in the dust. She twists and turns but can't work loose. And little by little Mitzi loosens her hold and looks at Kitty, now lying totally still with shiny red eyes.

Mitzi feels like laughing and combing the dark, dusty curls. But she controls herself and remains sitting, calm and silent, while she watches Kitty's movements as though she were taming an animal. And very slowly she lets her head sink down again to Kitty's heart which calms down little by little.

"Kitty-cat—" she whispers and her hand strokes the soft curls. "I like you a lot—say that you like me, too—"

"I love you," grunts Kitty. "You have any candy?"

"You're boring," mumbles Mitzi. "You only said it because of the candy—" And her hand is calm and warm on Kitty's collarbone and throat.

"Cross my heart—I can hardly breathe—"

Mitzi opens the heart-shaped purse and lets a bag drop to the ground.

Kitty snatches it up and stuffs her mouth.

"Not all of them—"mumbles Mitzi and grabs the half-empty bag. "You're crazy—The way you fill yourself up with coca-cola and candy—"

"Oh—" sighs Kitty with her mouth full. "Nothing'll happen. It's just normal poison—"

"Your teeth will fall out—"

"Not all of them at the same time," smiles Kitty, unassailable in her security. "Oh—I was completely hollow inside—" And her body shudders a bit from distaste.

"Don't you people ever cook?"

"Yes—of course," says Kitty self-importantly. "My mother's gone to a cooking school for young, well-educated women. We were supposed to have fish in seaweed with little synthetic lobster tails.—You know the ones that taste like cotton.—But the last three days my Dad's fish has had a spot on it. And then he throws out the entire dinner. Yesterday the sirens started bawling at the same time. And my mother bawled. And I bawled. We sat down in the basement, the three of us, bawling—until it was over."

"Just think—you bawled—" says Mitzi dreamily. "We had such a nice time.—We sat down in the party room and ate mice."

"Mice!" screams Kitty and jerks away, "Mice!—You people really are crazy."

"Mmm—They were innocent mice—white mice—untouched by human hands.—My dad works for a laboratory. He smuggles them out. You can't imagine what mice are like.—It's like eating newfallen snow.—They make you so clean."

And Mitzi lets herself roll around in the dust as though she were a white sensual snowflake.

"You're lucky—" says Kitty. "You're just lucky—You've got breasts—You don't have any problems at school—You don't have any problems at home—You're well-fed—And even your parents can put up with you."

"My Dad thinks I'm beautiful."

"You are.—You know sometimes I can't stand it.—Like yesterday in the basement—Suddenly I feel like I have to run or shout. My legs—they get all full of energy—they prickle—I just can't keep them still.—But there's no room to run. So I just stand there and kick and kick—And they can't stand it—They say they're going to have a button installed on me—so that they can turn me off like the washing machine and the TV—And if someone invents a button like that, then they'll push it all the way in, so that I just stand there and hum a bit like a test picture. Everything will go right through me.—I'll just be sort of a little wrong sound in the air—And nobody will miss me.—Not at school, either. Because I can't sit still. The words just turn into pricking in my legs. And I don't understand them."

"What is it—you don't understand?" Mitzi crushes a perfumed lozenge with her sharp white teeth.

Kitty quotes in a heavy nasal voice: "She looked at him over the tray with the round iced cakes. She couldn't swallow a thing. She was happy."

" 'Happy,'—is that the same as nausea?"

Mitzi shakes her head. "No—It's something for adults.—It's something they think they are or something they think they lack.—It's mostly something to do with belief."

"So it belongs to religion," Kitty concludes with surprise.

"No—you couldn't say that. It's more like consumption. Partners and consumption."

Kitty looks down in the dust and screams.

Very slowly a little round red insect comes strolling towards them.

You're crazy—" mumbles Mitzi. "That's a ladybug—just a ladybug." And she sticks out her finger, invitingly, towards it.

"It's got spots," whispers Kitty and pulls away. "Black spots."

"That's how ladybugs are.—They're supposed to have spots.—Ladybug—Ladybug—fly away home." And the little insect crawls slowly and hesitantly up onto the fingernail which Mitzi has painted green.

"Can you eat it?"

"Cannibal." She cups her hand protectively over the ladybug's round, matronly body. "Only birds eat ladybugs.—Rare birds.—People are only allowed to whisper to them. And blow on them. And set them free."

"Can I try?" asks Kitty. She jumps up and down and makes motor sounds with her lips.

"Ladybugs aren't meant for cannibals. Ladybugs aren't meant for

125

people who snivel and can't keep up." Mitzi hums giddily. "Maybe I'll keep it. It's almost as pretty as a horse. And someday when I'm in the right mood I'll blow on it."

She blows very gently.

The ladybug remains sitting on her skin as though it were glued there.

"You're a lazy ladybug—Awfully lazy.—Ladybugs can't fly."

And she fills her lungs and blows until the insect falls off her finger and lands on its back in the dust.

"It couldn't," gloats Kitty. "It was sick. I said it had spots. I could smell that it was sick."

She kicks Kitty hard in the shins to make her be quiet.

Then she resolutely opens the first aid kit.

She powders her finger. She powders the insect and the ground around the insect. She's on the verge of crying. But she grits her teeth and pulls up the white mask.

Then the alarm sounds and they run in separate directions.

Kitty drags one leg a bit. She stoops far forward, either because of her haste or because she's about to cry.

The soldier doll with its flame-thrower and the slender mannequin doll lie forgotten in the dust.

DORRIT WILLUMSEN

Born in 1940, the Danish author Dorrit Willumsen has produced over ten books: novels, short stories and poetry. She has achieved a steadily growing critical acclaim and popular success and in 1981 received the Grand Prize of the Danish Academy. She is influenced by both the writers of the absurd and the feminist movement, but her stories and style are her own. The collection of stories *If It Really Were A Film* was first published in Danish in 1978, and it deals with the situation of women from ancient Rome to the future. Indeed, Ms. Willumsen feels compelled to write another version (or vision) of Strindberg's play, which she calls "The Stronger II".

If It Really Were A Film is one of the fifteen books selected by the Danish component of Scandinavia Today to represent the finest in contemporary Danish literature.